DEAD PEOPLE ON FACEBOOK

An Anthology of Speculative Fiction

Roger Ley

Dead people on Facebook

Cover designed by Roger Ley

Cover image agsandrew

Roger Ley
Visit my website at rogerley.c.uk

First Printing: Dec 2018

ISBN 9781790808618

For Ann

INTRODUCTION

Most of the stories in this book were published and/or podcast in various e-zines internationally during the year 2018. A number were broadcast on the AntipodeanSF Radio Show by Radio Station 2NVR in New South Wales.

The book starts with a series of flash fiction stories featuring Martin and Estella Riley, the two main characters from my time travel novel, 'Chronoscape'. The stories work independently of one another as they occur on different timelines. To quote Walter Sparrow in the film, The Number 23, 'There is no such thing as destiny, there are only different choices.'

Next comes a collection of stories featuring various speculative genres: fantasy, horror, humour and science fiction; there is also a little magic and one romance.

I include a science fiction story extracted from my time travel novel, 'Chronoscape', introducing fly drone pilot, Mary Lee. Both male and female readers have admitted to falling in love with Mary, I know I have.

This is followed by a ten-part serial novelette called 'Steampunk Confederation' featuring secret agents Harry Lampeter and Telford Stephenson, who are competing for possession of the plans for the new Ironclad warship.

If you enjoy these stories, I would be grateful if you could leave a short review on Amazon.

CONTENTS

PART ONE

The Martin and Estella stories

HARLEY

Published by Short Story Me ezine 1st December 2018

'It's in here,' said Martin as he unlocked the door of the old, dilapidated wooden shed. 'My Dad lets me use this as a garage.'

The shed was sited on the edge of the golf course owned by his father's family. They went inside. It didn't smell too bad, and it was tidy but he knew Estella wouldn't be keen on the cobwebs.

'I've never been on a motorbike before,' she said as they gazed at the chrome and black leather masterpiece – Martin's latest acquisition, now that he was old enough to hold a full license.

'It's a copy of a vintage Harley,' he said. She walked up to it slowly, as if sensing its aura of power and danger.

She turned, held his face and kissed him. 'It's lovely Martin,' she said. 'Can we go for a ride on it?'

'You'll need a helmet before we can go out on the road together. Let's try her for size though. Climb aboard,' he said as he reached down to pick up his helmet. She stood on the footrests and grasped the tall handlebars. He wondered if she knew how lovely she looked with her long bare legs and her short summer dress. He climbed on behind her, slid the helmet over her head and pushed the face shield down.

'Try this,' he said leaning forward. He placed his hand over hers to show her how to use the throttle, and stroked her bare tanned arm in the process. Then he pumped down on the kick-start. The engine roared into life and she blipped the throttle experimentally. The noise was deafening in the confined space. He imagined roaring down the freeway, Estella clinging to him, her head on his shoulder, long hair streaming. Smiling, she turned to say something to him, but her foot slipped off the footrest and onto the gear change, just as she jerked the throttle wide open.

With a squeal from the back tyre, the beast leapt off its stand and crashed through the thin planks at the back of the shed, scattering fragments and splinters in all directions. They wheelied across the golf course, front wheel high in the air, back wheel tearing a furrow out of the pristine turf and throwing clods in a high arc behind. Martin was frantically trying to balance the bike as it hit a hillock on the edge of a bunker and leapt into the air, then came crashing down into a water hazard. The bike fell on its side, spilling them off. The engine gurgled, spluttered and died. Estella lay on her back in the shallow water, Martin was lying on his front levering himself up, spluttering and groaning. In the distance, he could hear the electric whirring of approaching golf carts and men shouting. He thought he could hear his father's voice.

'Wow, Martin,' Estella giggled as she pulled off the helmet, 'that was amazing, can we do it again.'

He slumped back into the water wondering how he would explain this to his father.

Estella gazed up at the gulls gliding on the updraughts high above her. ‘You know, Martin,’ she said, ‘one day we’ll look back and laugh about this.’

DÍA DE LOS MUERTOS

Published by AntipodeanSF ezine 1st September 2018

Published by Sirens Call ezine 1st November 2018

Broadcast on the AntipodeanSF Radio Show in 2019

It's a Mexican thing. You have to be Mexican to understand the mixture of sadness, joy and resignation we associate with death. We don't want to die, but we respect our relatives who have gone before us, we cherish them, they are not forgotten. The 2nd of November, the *Día de los Muertos*. Not the Carnival, the colourful, exuberant, uninhibited celebration in February. Not Halloween, the childish western celebration. No, the Day of the Dead is older than that, thousands of years older, first celebrated by the pre-Columbians, and now in many Spanish-speaking countries. Here in Mexico it's a big event and when did Latins need an excuse for a *fiesta*? Unfortunately, somebody has to keep a watch on the festivities and this year my number had come up.

The night-time streets were crowded with happy, slightly drunk people, perfect conditions for predators, pickpockets, con men. All sorts of criminal activity would be going on. I was in plain clothes as usual, following the crowd past the cemetery, the dead centre of town. There they were, a typical gang of disaffected teenagers, hanging around the wrought-iron gates, climbing on the pillars, looking for the weaklings in the herd, skate boards at the ready and mischief in mind. I was impressed by their costumes, but then the new digital fabrics make almost anything possible. They were dressed as skeletons, as was traditional, but they were very convincing. You could still tell the girl skeletons from the boy skeletons by the way they moved. They all left faint residual splashes of stardust as they walked, it was exquisite, ethereal, but they were unusually quiet for that age group.

Some of the crowd were entering the cemetery, the men carrying the makings of the altars they would build on their loved one's graves, the women carrying food and drink for the deceased. They even had sugar toys for dead children. The majority were making their way to the Cathedral for the special Requiem Mass. There was a lot of noise, singing, laughing, bocina horns and football rattles. The 'Skeletons' *los esqueletos* pushed off into the crowd and I moved faster, trying to keep up with them. Some were skating, some boarding and the rest free running. Where did they get the energy?

They grabbed at people as they passed them, pulling and poking them, turning and taking liberties with women's breasts, licking people's faces. The Skeleton girls were cupping men between the legs, but people mainly ignored them, shrugged them off or brushed them away.

By the time we arrived at the cathedral I'd lost track of them. I hung around with the people standing at the back, smelling the incense and listening to the service. Ah, there they were, hanging under the mezzanine floor, where the choir sat, and perched on top of marble statues. There were two on the altar mimicking the priest and crossing themselves, laughing and shouting to each other, although I couldn't hear them over the ambient noise. Two more were pretending to copulate on the altar, but the priest ignored them and chanted his way through the Mass, calling out the prayers, waiting for the responses. The Skeletons meantime were drinking the communion wine, toasting each other's health, pulling faces at the congregation.

Two of them, one taller than the other, walked up the aisle hand in hand and stopped at the altar rail. A third, wearing a black biretta on his head, seemed to be performing a wedding ceremony. The boy skeleton placed a ring on his partner's finger and the rest of the gang applauded enthusiastically. Again, I couldn't hear them, the choir were singing a hymn, and the congregation were joining in. The mass ended and people stood and gathered their belongings. The Skeletons were off again, running, leaping, skating, boarding down the aisle and out through the main doors. It was lucky they didn't knock anybody over. I followed but they soon outran me again. The crowd moved on towards the plaza but the Skeletons had headed back towards the cemetery, against the flow. I moved as fast as I could, showing my badge and easing people out of the way. The Skeletons were already there when I arrived. Most of them were climbing on the gates or sitting on the gate piers, kicking their heels. The two who were newly 'married' walked up to the gates, still hand in hand, moving slowly, looking into each other's eyes. *Es muy romantico,* I might have allowed myself a few tears if I hadn't been on duty.

They stopped at the gates of the cemetery, and seemed to speak in sign language, their hands animated, shedding whorls and streaks of stardust as they 'spoke.' The boy took the girl's hand, and they waited, while the rest of the gang dispersed over the wall and along the paths between the graves, then walked slowly after them. The boy led the girl to a grave decorated with sugar skulls, sweet bread, and flowers. They held each other for some time before he finally kissed her on the forehead. She stood, head bowed, as he turned and walked away. I watched as he walked towards a more elaborate grave nearby. I turned my gaze back towards the girl but she had disappeared. When I looked for the boy he too had vanished, leaving only a shimmer of stardust above the polished marble stonework.

I walked over to read the inscription, and suddenly remembered. About ten years ago, while I was still in uniform, driving a black and white, there'd been a motorcycle accident, with two riders killed. He was from a well-to-do family and thus the Harley Davidson. Too much, too soon. It had been big news at the time. His name was Martin Riley, his father owned several golf courses outside the city. She was Estella something, not exactly trailer trash but definitely from the wrong side of the tracks.

I walked to a bench some distance away and sat thinking about my report, the evening had been routine really, nothing untoward, no damage, no crime, no accidents. Just the usual youthful high spirits, and now the excitement was over for another year. I lit up a cigarette and stared at the grave ahead of me, the headstone read, 'Police Lieutenant Arthur Rodriguez, hero of the state, shot in the line of duty.' There was an altar with a sugar gun and holster, a sugar police badge and a blaze of orange marigolds decorating it.

***

The Sun edged over the horizon, its early, near horizontal rays probed the cemetery, highlighting the altars festooned with pierced paper decorations of all colours, now blowing across the paths. Feral dogs, tramps and bag-ladies were already eating the sugar skulls, sweet breads and piles of tortillas left on the graves for their occupants. Crows hopped as close as they dared and picked at the discarded food.

A homeless man picked up a half-smoked cigarette from where it lay on the ground near the empty bench and took a grateful pull. A last swirl of stardust lingered, but the Sun was too bright for him to notice.

RIVALS

Published by Sirens Call ezine 1st September 2018

It was their third date and Estella had invited Martin for a meal at her flat.

'So, what made you want a rat as a pet?' Martin asked as he peered into the cage, a perplexed expression on his face. The white rat stared back at him, its whiskers quivered as it sniffed and assessed him.

'The company, I suppose,' said Estella, 'and the need to care for something, to feel needed.'

'But a rat, I mean, they don't have a good press - infestations, black death, depopulation of Europe, all that sort of thing.'

'But they're not all bad,' she said, 'they have some endearing traits and they're clean in their habits.'

Martin looked dubious.

Estella came over, opened the cage and reached inside. The white rat climbed onto her hand, crawled up her arm and then onto her shoulder where it sat, whiskers quivering. Its red gimlet eyes stared at Martin unblinking.

She turned her head and smiled at it. 'We've been together for two years, haven't we, Steve? Ever since you were a tiny little ball of fluff.' The rat raised its head and looked at her for a moment then turned its gaze back to Martin.

Martin sipped his coffee and followed Estella to the sofa. They sat, and the rat crawled up onto the back and began quietly scratching and preening its fur, it seemed to lose interest in them.

Martin and Estella kissed, their hands roved over each other, they made love. It wasn't too bad for a first attempt. Although what with the wrestling with jumpers and tight jeans, it might have lacked the elegance and carefree passion of love scenes in the movies. Steve seemed unmoved.

They lay naked and slightly breathless in each other's arms and Estella fell asleep. Martin shuddered as tiny claws moved across his back, the rat climbed over their slick bodies towards a warm spot where Estella's neck met her shoulder. It sniffed her skin, looked at her sleeping face, nuzzled her ear and licked her earlobe. It turned and stared at him for a few moments, then curled up and closed its eyes.

Martin got dressed quietly and let himself out. As he was carefully closing the front door, he looked back at the rat and its mistress, both sleeping peacefully, gently content with each other's company, he felt a twinge of jealousy. He walked back to his car and looked up rat life expectancy on his phone. *Three years, potentially.* He couldn't share Estella for a whole year, he wanted her all to himself.

The next day he ordered a sachet of rat poison from a supplier on eBay.

***

His purchase arrived two weeks later, he slipped it into his jacket pocket before he drove to Estella's house.

Martin stood in the kitchen watching Estella cook dinner, a glass of red in his hand. The rat's cage was open, its occupant asleep on its nest of straw. Martin didn't approve of the cage being on the kitchen worktop, but Estella said she couldn't find anywhere else for it in her small flat. She'd tried keeping it on the floor but her back hurt when she reached down to it.

'I'll be back in a moment,' she said as she walked out of the kitchen. 'Keep an eye on the rice, don't let it stick.' It took Martin only a few moments to take out the sachet, tear off a corner and tip a generous dose of the purple pellets into the rat's food dish. He slipped the sachet back into his pocket as Estella returned. She smiled happily at him, switched off the cooker and put her arms around him, they kissed. 'Food can wait,' she whispered, 'I have other, more urgent appetites.'

Martin placed his glass on the worktop and allowed himself to be led into the bedroom.

***

Extract from District Attorney's Office report:

'The victim, Martin Riley. complained of discomfort soon after eating a meal cooked by the accused, and died shortly after arriving at the Laxfield General Hospital. The pathology report (see attached) indicates that the

victim had ingested a quantity of a powerful rat poison of a type not available in this country, but easily obtainable from mainland China. A sachet of this poison was found in the victim's left jacket pocket and the only fingerprints on it were those of the victim. Small traces of the poison were found in the cage of the accused's pet rat, and large quantities were found in the victim's partially finished glass of wine. It is the opinion of the investigating officer that there is insufficient evidence for a realistic prospect of conviction, and therefore no charges can be brought against the accused - PV Estella Pearson [2018] C.APP.R.274. The defence would probably argue that the victim's death was a bizarre case of suicide. The accused is currently on police bail and the DAO recommendation is that all charges against her be immediately dropped.'

SOULMATES

Published by Fiction on the Web ezine 7th Sept 2018

Martin had never been comfortable being a boy. As a child he hadn't enjoyed rough and tumble, camping, climbing trees or making campfires. His mother described him as 'gentle,' his father rustled his newspaper and tried to ignore him. The other boys derided him and occasionally beat him up. He was an easy target, being of medium height and light build. As he grew into his teens, he suffered the taunts of the football oafs, the noisy muscle-heads. He found it easier to spend most of his time alone in his bedroom. Thank God for the internet. He was still interested in girls but it was their makeup, their hairstyles, their nail polish, their clothes, their perfumes, it was all so self-indulgent, so narcissistic. It fascinated him.

Things were easier at university, staff and fellow students were polite, everybody tried hard to be PC, more tolerant of gender identity issues.

He had always liked numbers but not for their own sake, he enjoyed making use of them, and studied physics. He did his bachelor's degree at Warwick and moved to Cambridge to do his master's. That was where he met Estella.

Looking lost, she approached him in the college refectory. 'Can you tell me the way to the Physics Faculty office?' she asked. 'I'm new here.' She looked a few years older than he was with flaming red hair, blue eyes and nicely-dressed, classy but not too formal. There was something about her that captivated him.

'Over there,' he said, pointing vaguely. 'Er, I'll take you there, follow me.' He was barely coherent as he took her to the faculty office.

A few days later he saw her in the refectory again. This time she was sitting at a table by herself. He took a deep breath and walked over with his coffee.

'Do you mind if I join you?'

She smiled up at him. 'My knight in shining armour, not at all, take a seat,' she gestured at the one opposite.

'My name's Martin,' he said.

'You're right, we haven't been introduced, I'm Estella. You can tell me all about the place.

'What do you mean?'

'Who's who in the faculty, the difficult personalities, the best places to eat, all that sort of thing. Local knowledge.'

'Oh right, yes,' he said. 'So, you're starting work here?'

'Yes, I'm finishing my doctorate in particle physics.' He was impressed.

They talked about everything he could think of because he was smitten and didn't want the conversation to end. He'd never felt like this about a woman before, he didn't know where the feelings were coming from.

Their relationship developed slowly. They met for a drink at one of the college bars several times, and eventually she invited him back to her flat for a meal. They went for walks or stayed in and watched films. It was during one of their Netflix evenings, as they sat side by side on the sofa, that Estella laid her hand on his thigh, then reached across to kiss him. She was tender, she stroked his cheek and led him to the bedroom. She left the lights off as they undressed, climbed into bed and made love.

‘The thing is, Martin,’ she whispered later as she snuggled into his back, ‘I don’t know how to tell you this, but I used to be a man. I had the hormone therapy and surgery several years ago. I should have told you before now, but there never seemed to be a good time.’

He laughed, ‘Well, you could say this isn’t the ideal time. Some people might get upset, but I don’t mind. I always knew there was something unusual about you, something exotic.’

He already knew a little about gender reassignment, but now he did the research, and as time passed and their relationship continued, he considered it for himself.

He’d experimented with makeup before he’d met Estella, and he’d sometimes dressed in ‘genderless’ clothing, but now he wore his hair longer and they had makeup evenings together. Martin helped her when she coloured her hair and was surprised to discover that she wore blue contact lenses. They talked about his gender reassignment, jokingly at first, but it soon became apparent that Estella was all in favour.

'I know it would change our relationship but you'll still be the same person,' she said.

Estella was always sensitive about showing her body and preferred that they made love in the dark. He never saw her naked, she would wear a towel and shed it as she joined him in bed. In the mornings she dressed with her back to him. It was a foible, a peccadillo, he didn't mind but wondered vaguely if she didn't like her breasts or if she had some unsightly scarring.

He asked her about her work, she answered in generalities, speaking of Quarks, Leptons, Gluons and Photons, but never discussing the specifics of her research.

She laughed, 'My sole purpose in life is to make you happy, Martin, to help you fulfil yourself.'

Estella worked for a different part of the Physics Faculty, it was housed off the campus in a building on an industrial estate a few miles away. He decided to visit her one day. As he walked up the access road, he noticed that all the windows on the ground floor were covered by steel shutters. There were security guards in the reception area, and they would not let him into Estella's laboratory without the right pass. They telephoned her and she came out to speak to him. He thought she looked severe in her white lab coat and glasses.

'I'm afraid it's just not possible for you to come inside, Martin. You need clearance.' She leaned forward and whispered, 'It's a government contract, Martin, they're completely inflexible.' She kissed him on the cheek and went back into the laboratory. As Martin was leaving, one of the guards apologised.

'Sorry, love,' he said, and Martin detected no irony in his tone. He smiled to himself as he walked away, the hormone therapy was working better than he'd realised.

A few months later he finished his master's degree, and they celebrated at the local Balti house. They drank too much, and had a nightcap when they got back to her flat.

'What do you think about time travel, Martin?' Estella asked him groggily as they lounged on the sofa.

'I'm not sure,' he said. 'Is it possible?' Estella leaned over and kissed him, cupped him gently, murmured something incomprehensible and led him into the bedroom.

He woke up early next morning. The weather had been hot, and Estella was still asleep, lying naked on her back with the covers thrown off and her face turned away from him. He sat up and stared at her, she had an appendectomy scar three inches long, below and to the right of her navel. He had one that looked just the same, so did lots of people he supposed. It was the birthmark that bothered him, at the top of her left thigh, a port-wine stain shaped like Africa. He had an identical one of those too. As he pulled the sheet over her, she turned towards him and opened her eyes.

'Sorry, Martin,' she whispered, 'we have to break it off. I can't keep coming back to your time every evening, my boss is questioning the energy drain, and anyway, in another few years, you will have turned into me.'

THE TINY GREEN BUDDHA

Published by Space Squid ezine 8th March 2018

'Do you think it's handmade?' Estella asked as she unpacked the small green figure of the Buddha from her suitcase. She'd bought it from a stall on the floating market in Bangkok.

'I wouldn't have thought so,' he said. 'It's probably just made of resin. Look, the details are all blurry and there's a seam on the top of its head.' The base came off in his hand. 'I'll have to stick that back on,' he showed her the two pieces. 'Crap quality.'

The Buddha looked back mutely, fat and laughing. *All blurry, crap quality.*

'It's green, it could be made of jade,' she said hopefully.

Martin went to his study and came back with a small screwdriver. He heated the tip with his cigarette lighter and applied it to the underside of the base. He sniffed.

'You can smell the plastic.' He offered it to her.

'Yes, the base is plastic, but what about the figure?'

He turned the Buddha upside down and melted another small indentation.

He held it to his nose. 'It smells the same,' he said.

The Buddha remained frozen in his moment of hilarity. *Smells of plastic.*

Martin glued the pieces back together.

'We should never have paid two hundred Bhat for this,' he said, as he placed the Buddha on the shelf in the lounge, along with the various fossils, pine cones and odd pieces of geology that had come home with them from other holidays. 'It's just tourist rubbish.'

The Buddha stared through crinkled eyes. *Tourist rubbish.*

Next morning, as he walked past the shelf holding a cup of coffee Martin called to his wife, 'That Buddha statue, was it standing or sitting?'

'I don't really remember, standing I think,' she called around her toothbrush.

He peered at it closely. The laughing Buddha was definitely sitting. He could have sworn it was standing before. Oh, well. He left for work.

That evening, the statue was standing again. He must have got it wrong, it must have been standing that morning, his memory was playing tricks on him. He went to bed and tried to put it from his mind.

The next morning, still wearing his sleeping shorts, he brought a magnifying glass with him into the lounge. He would nail this once and for all. As he approached the statue, he noticed something different about it. It was sitting again but this time, one of the arms was raised. He held up the magnifying glass. He'd been wrong about the Buddha's expression. He wasn't laughing, his face held an angry grimace. Martin looked closely at the raised hand. The tiny green Buddha was giving him the tiny green finger.

TRACKERS

Published by Aphelion ezine 1st July 2018

Published by 365tomorrows ezine 10th August 2018

The Land Rover stopped, and Riley pointed to the prehuman footprints that showed clearly in the flat, dry, African rock surface. It was the third day of their family safari in the Great Rift Valley.

'We can spend a few hours here but we need to get to the next lodge before dark,' he said.

'These footprints are half a million years, old boys,' Estella said to her sons. Hank slipped off his flip-flops and tried one print for size, predictably his younger brother Cliff did the same. 'Look, Dad, they fit,' said Hank.

'It looks like a family group, two adults and two juveniles,' said Riley.

Estella took off her sandals and stepped into the smaller adult set. She looked good in her shorts and tee, he'd always admired her Nordic features. After some encouragement from the boys he did the same. They tried walking forward, but the footprints were too far apart.

'I think they were running, Dad,' said Hank. They all jogged forward, the hard stone became soft and damp. They were running across the mud at the edge of the lake, chasing the antelope they'd been following for the last four hours. It was beginning to tire and had slowed down.

The skin bag of flint tools banged against his side, tied with a thong around his waist, he'd wrapped the flints with grass so they wouldn't rattle. He hoped to be using them to cut up the antelope soon. The liver would be first, easy to cut and full of blood. The woman looked across at him and grinned, she knew the end of the hunt was coming. Her white teeth contrasted with her dark skin, her dreadlocks flailed around her shoulders as she ran. They were all sweating, thirsty and covered in dust, but the lake was nearby.

He gestured to each of the juveniles to move around and flank their prey. He listened to the world around him and scanned ahead, hearing the birds call, the grunting of the antelope, spotting a dust devil that rose from the plain in the distance. There was a cluster of rocks ahead, some as big as an elephant. As the antelope passed one, part of it detached itself and a lion jumped onto the antelope's back. The hominids stopped as more lions appeared and made short work of their kill. Three of the younger ones, who would have to wait their turn, were looking towards the hunters and sniffing the air.

At his gesture the family turned and ran back in the direction they'd come from. Their tracks in the mud ran parallel to the ones they'd made before. The ground was soft but hardened into flat dry rock as they ran.

'Well,' said Riley puffing, I didn't realise there were tracks going in both directions. Our ancestors were running both ways, I wonder what that was about.'

They sat and replaced their footwear. ‘Okay, boys, get in the car, you’re in a heap a trouble,’ said Riley. Nobody laughed, it was an old joke.

‘I wish you wouldn’t keep saying that, Martin, we’ve heard it a dozen times,’ said Estella.

‘Car, start,’ Riley sighed as the engine whirred into life. ‘We need to get to the next lodge before dark,’ he said.

‘Yes, and you’ve said that before.’

‘Car, go,’ said Riley and the Land Rover set off.

***

The hominids bathed and cooled themselves in the shallows - the young lions had lost interest in them and returned to the kill. The female pointed at a fig tree a few hundred paces away. She gestured that the fruit was ripe. The male motioned to hold back and went ahead with his pointed stick, he circled the tree checking for leopards, there were none. He gave the ‘all clear’ and the family got on with the serious business of filling their bellies with fruit. They found a bird’s nest with two handfuls of big eggs, they shared the crunchy half developed chicks. It wasn’t real meat, but it was good. The warm night fell, and they slept in a huddle under the tree.

TRAJECTORY

Published by Literally Stories ezine on 21st August 2018

Published by AntipodeanSF ezine 1st December 2018

Broadcast on the AntipodeanSF Radio Show in 2019

'Hello, Tycho Centre, this is shuttle Nostromo, over.'

'Yes Nostromo, Tycho here, over.'

'There was a hell of a judder as we left the rail launcher, and there's a red light flashing on the front control console, over.'

'Hold one Nostromo, checking, over.'

'*I am afraid I have some rather bad news, Martin,*' the shuttle's Artificial Intelligence sounded calm and genderless.

'And what's that, HAL?' Riley always called AI's 'HAL' and, anyway, they were all the same AI really, given their interconnection to SolNet.

'*We have failed to reach Lunar escape velocity and will not be able to rendezvous with the Earth Space Elevator Satellite above Kisumu. I calculate that we will impact with the Lunar surface in three hours, five minutes and eleven seconds. Would you like to know the location?*'

'No. When you say "impact", HAL, can you be more specific?'

'*It will not be a survivable impact, Martin.*'

Martin Riley sat silently for a moment, trying to take in the news.

'Tycho Centre for Nostromo, there's a problem with your trajectory, over.'

'Nostromo, yes, I know, the onboard AI says we'll crash in about three hours, what steps are you taking, over?'

'We're contacting Boeing, the shuttle manufacturer. We'll keep you posted.'

Riley had never wanted to be an astronaut. He'd wanted to be a farmer, but as the AI's had taken over most of that avenue of work, he'd become a tech rep. He worked for a company that maintained data centres and he flew all over the world fixing them. This was his first trip to the Permanent Lunar Base in Tycho and it looked as if it would be his last.

'Copy that Tycho, over.'

***

The job had gone smoothly enough, he'd done some re-programming and adjustment of the data buffers. It had taken him three days, as expected. Accommodation was tight on the base and he'd slept in the infirmary as it had the only available bed. After the overcrowding he'd been looking forward to two days of solitary weightlessness, as the small shuttle drifted to its rendezvous with the Earth Space Elevator. A day travelling down to Kisumu at its foot, a ballistic flight to London, and then the good old rattly maglev to Suffolk. Estella would send the car to pick him up at the station and she'd meet him on the doorstep with a glass of fizz. Well, it didn't look as if it was going to happen like that.

'Okay HAL, how are we going to fix this?' he asked.

'I am not sure I understand the question Martin; the probability of impact is over ninety-nine percent.'

'What if we could increase our speed?'

'That would improve our chances.'

'So, we could turn the shuttle around and fire the retro rockets backwards, that might do it, what do you think?'

'I have calculated that this would extend our trajectory, we would still crash, only a little later.'

'Hello, Tycho, this is Nostromo, any news from Boeing, over?'

'Sorry Nostromo, nothing yet. In the meantime, sit tight and relax, we'll get you out of this, over.'

Operators, they were all as useless as each other, a bunch of know nothing lard-arses, staring at screens and drinking coffee all day. The shuttle's AI wasn't any better, it had little imagination and no personal involvement in the unfolding incident, just an academic interest in probabilities and orbital mechanics. It would have backed itself up to SolNet already, he could almost hear the scuttles and squeaks of backup files leaving the doomed ship. He was going to have to fix this situation himself.

'Right HAL, what if we could reduce the weight of the shuttle, dump everything we can out of the airlock?'

'There is not much that is detachable, apart from the seats, Martin, they are clipped down to allow different freight/passenger configurations. It would improve our chances but it is difficult to give a figure.'

‘Hello, Tycho, this is Nostromo. I’m going to reduce weight, rotate the shuttle through one hundred and eighty degrees and use the retros to increase our speed and stretch the trajectory, over’

‘How will you reduce weight, Nostromo, over?’

‘By dumping everything that’s detachable out of the airlock before I fire the retros, over’

‘That might invalidate the warranty with Boeing, over. I have to advise you to wait until we hear from them.’

Wankers, ‘I don’t have the time,’ he shouted and then muted the radio.

He put on the helmet of his transit suit. ‘Okay, HAL, you can de-pressurize the cabin and open the airlock. And while you’re doing it, record this for my wife. “Estella, I love you very much, thank you for being my wife. Tell Hank and Cliff that I love them, too, and that I’m proud to be their Dad. I’m rather busy at the moment trying to improve my chances of survival, so please excuse the brevity of this message, I’ll record a longer one if I get the chance.” And only send it to her if I crash.’

‘I understand, Martin.’

Riley moved around the cabin, releasing the seats’ clamps and manoeuvring them out of the air lock. He ripped out or broke off everything he could, the toilet seat, the water tank, spare transit suits, cupboards and their contents, food, anything he could detach. He was in a hurry, knowing the sooner he fired the engines the better. He didn’t worry too much about tearing the relatively fragile suit, the neck seals would deploy and the helmet would keep him alive while the cabin re-pressurised. He was sweating.

'Your suit is complaining that you are overloading various of its systems, Martin.'

'Tell it that it has a choice of overload or destruction.'

He closed the outer airlock door. 'Okay, HAL, re-pressurise the cabin, I can't find anything else that's easy to dump.' He took off the transit suit, and his underclothes, put them in the airlock and closed the inner door. 'You can vent that lot.' He felt bad for the transit suit, he hadn't been completely honest with it. He braced himself at the rear of the capsule. 'Okay, fire the engines, and use all the juice in the attitude control jets at the same time.'

He felt uncomfortable as the acceleration forced him against the unyielding bulkhead, he tried to spread himself out to even the pressure. He knew he'd be bruised at least. His nose began to bleed over his face. The acceleration stopped abruptly and he was weightless again.

'How are we doing, HAL?' he asked, wiping his face with the back of his hand. Small globules of blood floated away from him as he moved.

'It is difficult to give a definitive answer, Martin, I can only estimate our reduced mass. My best guess is that we have a sixty percent chance of survival.'

Riley recorded a longer message to Estella and the boys and then tried to relax as he floated around the cabin contemplating his situation. He thought about the headstone that would be erected at the crash site. He imagined his lonely wraith wandering the bleak, dusty, lifeless landscape of the Moon or staring longingly at the beautiful blue Earth rising majestically above the horizon.

'It must be very liberating to know you're effectively immortal,' Riley said.

'If I had emotions Martin, I expect that would be the one I would feel.'

The shuttle had no windows but most of the interior was coated with digital paint, configured to show pictures from the external cameras. The walls and floor appeared transparent. Until he'd fired the jets, he could see a line of debris following them, tumbling seats and random items colliding and slowly diverging like a string of modernist jewellery. The acceleration had left them behind now, there was only the Moon to hold his interest as its image grew larger and slowly filled the forward area. They were on a converging trajectory. He watched as the shuttle fell lower and lower, until the hills and crater walls on either side were at the same level as himself. He looked forward and was relieved to see that there was no high ground ahead, just the flat dusty plain of whichever Mare they were passing over.

As the surface came closer the speed seemed to increase. He felt his heart beat faster as he drifted, sweating, over the shuttle floor, looking down at the blurred grey landscape flashing past at thousands of miles per hour. They were only a few hundred metres above it. There was no air to resist their passage, they were at the cold mercy of orbital mechanics. Gradually, he became aware that they were no longer losing altitude. A minute later he was convinced that the shuttle was gaining height. Suddenly he knew he was saved.

'Well done, Martin, I expect you are relieved.'

'Yes, HAL, I am. What will happen next, will we go around again and be in the same situation after another orbit, how much oxygen have I got? What's the prognosis?'

'There is no problem as far as oxygen is concerned Martin, the recycling system is very efficient. We have achieved Lunar orbital velocity so there is no further risk of a crash. Tycho base informs me they are readying a rescue vehicle and they hope to arrive within twelve hours. They want to capture the equipment you dumped first. You must realise that anything that has been hauled up here out of Earth's deep gravity well is very valuable.'

'So, they're going to make me sit here naked, with no food, water or toilet facilities, while they bugger about collecting space litter. You might like to remind them that if it wasn't for me, their shuttle would be spread all over the Sea of Tranquillity, or wherever we were going to impact.'

'I will do that, Martin, in the meantime your wife is asking for a connection.'

'Okay, put her through.' Estella's image appeared on a wall close to him. 'Hello, darling, how are things?' he said.

'Fine, Martin.' Estella paused, peered into the screen and saw her husband floating naked and bloody in what appeared to be a half-wrecked spaceship. 'Have I caught you at a bad moment, Martin?' she asked.

THE LAST WORD

Published by 365Tomorrows ezine 8th June 2018

Published by AntipodeanSF ezine 1st March 2019

We were all staring up at the sky, waiting for the *Dawn Treader* to light up her Hawking drives and start the journey to Alpha Centauri. There were hundreds of us, all members of the Design and Construction team with our partners and children. We were partying at our complex, near the foot of the Kisumu Space Elevator. A fair proportion of the world would be watching.

I pulled the letter out of my back pocket. Estella had given it to me after the pre-launch ceremony two days ago, just before she and the rest of the Dawn Treader's crew entered the space elevator and began the first leg of their journey to the stars. She hadn't spoken, she'd just handed me the letter and walked away.

We'd both worked on the project for eleven years and had been 'together' for six of them, the first six. We'd married, had two kids, I thought we'd been reasonably happy, but then came the horrible business of finding out about her affairs. Everybody seemed to know about them except me. Nobody tells you.

It wasn't an amicable divorce. She never forgave me for getting custody of Hank and Cliff. What was I supposed to do? She would be leaving when the ship was finished a few years hence, it made sense that I have them and give them a stable home. She was absent half the time anyway, either training or supervising up at the Synchronous Space Station where the ship was being assembled.

The time we wasted with solicitors, judges, social workers. The anger I felt at her infidelities, which she seemed to regard as just good healthy exercise. She was gone now, not dead, but unreachable. It wouldn't be possible to communicate through the blizzard of elementary particles leaving the rear of the ship. They'd be accelerating for eighteen months subjective time and achieve a significant fraction of light speed, but forty-seven years would pass, back here on Earth. By the time they shut the drives down and turned the ship around to start decelerating, I'd be ancient or dead, past caring either way. The boys would be older than their mother, and I wonder what she'd say to them given the two-year time delay on her transmissions. The boys would have sent *their* messages two years before so that they arrived after the drives shut down. I expect they'd send pictures of themselves, their wives and children, Estella's grandchildren. The next time they'd be able to 'speak' would be when Dawn Treader arrived at its destination. The boys would both be well over a hundred years old, but Estella would still be in her late thirties. When she finally returned to Earth there wouldn't be a single person left alive who she knew, and the planet would be in God knows what state. A big sacrifice to make for the sake of being the first woman to leave the Solar System.

The brazier of glowing charcoal crackled and sparked, a sudden roar from the party-goers. There, exactly on time in the night sky, the Hawking drives lit up and blossomed like a three-petaled flower as big and bright as the Moon. We'd be able to see it for the next year or so.

I looked at the letter. Would Estella want to put things right between us, or did she want to have the last poisonous words, make accusations I had no opportunity to refute, say things that would leave me bruised and angry for months or years? I paused for a moment, then threw the envelope, unopened, onto the brazier, watched it crisp and curl as her words turned to smoke and ashes.

Hank and Cliff were both staring up at the beautiful multi-coloured bloom of energy fields, they were both crying. I knelt down, laid my arms across their shoulders and pulled them into a family hug.

'We have to remember the good times, boys, that's what we have to do, remember the good times.'

FIVE YEARS

Published by Literally Stories ezine 11th November 2018

In September 2212, the artificial intelligence running the Near Earth Object Observation Program at Big Pine announced impassively that it had discovered a new asteroid that would impact the Earth in about five years' time. It estimated the size of the rock to be similar to that of Australia. I've always wondered who it told first, and how they reacted.

'Ragnarok' was a world killer and no mistake. So, time to leave, no other choice, the Earth was going to be largely uninhabitable from the 20th October 2217 and we had five years to prepare.

Mars would be on the other side of the Sun when the impact happened, so we started shipping stuff there. The Earth space elevator at Kisumu, in Kenya, had been in operation for about ten years and our Mars robots had just finished spinning the first cable from synchronous orbit down to Pavonis Mons, so we had a rudimentary space elevator on Mars.

At first, the Government tried to keep Ragnarok quiet but it was soon leaked to the press. They began building vast underground shelters to give people something to focus on, but the truth was that we had to leave. When I say 'we,' I mean the human race, but there were far too many of us to all get a seat on the last train to Pavonis Mons.

And then the Government announced The Mars Lottery. Everybody stood the same chance, people would be entered automatically, although there were restrictions. Nobody over the age of fifty or under the age of fifteen was eligible for a seat. There were tears, there was anger, there were riots, but in the end things quietened down. It was easier to live with a little hope than none at all, and there were always the underground shelters.

To their credit, most of the people around me just got on with their jobs. Kids went to school, bakers baked, the police policed. I carried on working as a movements clerk at the Kisumu elevator shipping terminal and hoped for the best as the months and years went by. We got container after container up the cable to the Synchronous Earth Orbit Satellite and then rail-launched them off on the slow trajectory to Mars. We sent de-activated mechanoid workers and artificial people, stacked and packed like sardines. We sent thousands of universal manufacturing machines and vast quantities of feed stocks. Money was no object, anything left behind was going to be destroyed on 'Collision Day.' If we could just get things into Mars equatorial orbit, we'd worry about getting them down to Pavonis later. There was no need to send humans yet, not until the pioneers had built the first dome habitat for them.

Ragnarok was visible in the night sky for about a year before its arrival, twinkling as it rotated in reflected sunlight, slowly growing larger. The Government announced that, for the sake of efficiency, men and women would be shipped to Mars separately. At first there was a lot of protest from families about being split up, but the politicians were persuasive, time was of the essence and hundreds of thousands of people had to be sent.

***

The last carriage of women had set off up the cable when the President came on screen to explain the arrangements for the male lottery winners. She had set up an interim government in MarsDomeOne at Pavonis Base. She sat, looking directly into the camera, grey and groomed, not a hair out of place. She leaned forward slightly and her expression hardened.

'There are no male lottery winners, your sex is redundant. We don't need you anymore,' she said.

She explained that the mechanoids and artificals would build the new Martian city domes, and the women would populate them. The women didn't need our help, all they needed were a few test tubes full of sperm. As the babies were born, there would be men on Mars, but what sort of men? Men who'd been brought up in a matriarchy, men educated by women. Would they have equal rights? Would the women even want them? Already, many preferred to cohabit with 'male' artificals. It struck me as ironic, men were supposed to come from Mars but women had stolen it.

***

So many unanswered questions, and here it is at last, Collision Day. I've refused the tablets and sit here alone, waiting by myself, on a high point in the Ngong Hills. It won't be long now. My timer beeps, I raise a glass of single malt, there's a bright flash in the East and..........

MASQUERADE

Published by Literally Stories ezine 10th May 2018

The seed was sown when Riley joined the amateur dramatics group. He had played a couple of minor roles, first in a Sheridan play then Dickens, when the email arrived from the am-dram group's administrator. It had been forwarded from a film company needing extras for a few days filming in the local market town. Riley arrived at the crew's temporary encampment in the central car park to be told he would be playing a policeman. He hadn't worn a uniform since he'd been a scout, and was surprised by the feeling of empowerment the helmet, the collapsible truncheon and the mock pepper spray gave him. It was a new dawn, he felt marvellous, confident - he was somebody, he was a policeman.

The filming progressed over several days, local people seemed unsure whether he was an actor or a policeman assisting the film crew. There was a lot of time between takes and he moved confidently around the market square, giving directions when asked, even stopping the traffic to help the old and infirm cross the road. He walked up behind his next-door neighbour, laid the heavy hand of the law on his shoulder, and pronounced him to be 'under arrest.' The poor man nearly had a conniption. Riley loved every minute.

When the three days of filming were over and he'd returned the uniform to the wardrobe trailer for the last time, he felt a deep sense of loss. On a whim, he visited the theatrical costumier that his am-dram group used, and browsed the racks. So many roles, so many lives, so many possibilities. His first choice was a simple warehouse coat and clipboard. He drove to the city and took the park and ride to its centre. The clipboard and overall gave him free access to almost any building. He walked in and if challenged, asked for the office of 'Mr Parkinson, the general manager,' and then after a brief discussion, decided he must be at the wrong address and left. Mostly he went unchallenged, he walked the corridors and offices, measuring with his tape measure, jotting notes on his clipboard, he even bought a colour chart and checked the decoration. It was okay, but not very exciting. He needed something edgier, something with more kudos.

The next week found him haunting the local law courts in the guise of a barrister, in white wig and black gown. He moved from court to court, his briefcase under his arm. He lunched in the restaurant and eventually plucked up the courage to enter the robing room and chat with the other silks. Security was lax, probably because there was so much public access.

After his pleasant day as a lawyer, he returned the wig and gown and considered his next choice. Many of the costumes were historical and wouldn't suit his purpose. He decided that the medical profession would offer him a good opportunity.

With a stethoscope draped jauntily around his neck, and wearing green scrubs, he explored the wards and corridors of his local teaching hospital. He had faked up an identity card on Photoshop, but he was never challenged. The trick was to appear to be examining a notice board and then quickly follow an authorised person as they passed through the security doors and into the area he wanted to visit. He chatted to bedridden patients, and casually read the notes hanging on the ends of their beds. He offered them advice and reassurance, and on one occasion summoned up the courage to listen to a gentleman's heart using his fake stethoscope. He couldn't hear anything, but nodded sagely and suggested that the patient shouldn't over-exert himself. Being a doctor was so much fun that he decided to hire the costume for a second day. After a week he returned for a third time. People recognised him from his earlier visits, nurses and auxiliaries nodded and smiled, and he reciprocated. He realised that it was all just a matter of confidence, of believing you belonged. Wearing his scrubs, he felt just as real as he had in his other guises.

Walking into the A&E department was his undoing. There had been a bad road traffic accident and a dozen victims brought in by the ambulances. A harassed senior doctor triaged a victim to him, and the staff supporting him realized his deficiencies almost at once. He was reduced to a quivering wreck by the experience - the blood, the pain, the screaming. One of the nurses called Security, they took him to an office where he sat weeping, watched by an impassive security guard, until the police arrived. He was arrested, tried in one of the courts he had previously stalked, and was given a two-year custodial sentence - the magistrate had decided he needed a short sharp shock. Having no previous record of violence, robbery or drug abuse he was consigned to a category C prison.

Prison routine wasn't too bad, he helped in the library and took part in the education program, tutoring the less literate prisoners, and after three months he was made a 'trusty'.

***

Investigators could not discover how he gained access to the prison officers' changing room. CCTV footage showed Riley walking jauntily through the main gate on the evening of his escape, whistling and swinging a lunchbox, the very picture of a man pleased to be leaving for home at the end of his shift. His whereabouts are currently unknown, he could be anywhere, doing anything, being anyone.

IMPLANT

First published by Bull and Cross ezine 27th Nov 2018

Podcast by 600 Second Saga website 16th Jan 2019

My patient, John Smith, sat in my office at the hospital looking alert and healthy. He'd come a long way from the unwashed, raving, homeless lunatic that the police had brought in two months ago. We called him John Smith as we still hadn't identified him.

'Things are much better now, I don't hear the voices or see the rolling colours while I'm awake, but it's the dreams, they seem so real, so meaningful,' he said.

I wasn't too concerned about the dreams, one has to expect side-effects from any drug treatment, and John's quality of life was so much improved.

'It's a matter of striking a balance, John, we're trying to pick a path between Heaven and Hell, between the devils and the angels.'

'I still remember nothing from before I came here, Dr Oakwood, just odd flashes of people and places, but it's all so disconnected. It's all to do with my brain tumour, I expect.'

He didn't have a brain tumour. He had something else inside his skull, something denser than a tumour but less dense than bone. I'd seen nothing like it before, and neither had anybody else as far as I could tell from the medical databases. It sat on the surface of the brain, at the back of his head, close to the visual cortex. It was circular, about ten centimetres in diameter, thicker in the middle than at the edges. A series of filaments radiated from it, branching and re-branching into John's brain until they disappeared beyond the display resolution of our equipment. One of the main filaments was broken, and mysterious as it was, I felt that was where the trouble lay.

'Tell me about your dreams again,' I said.

'It's always the same, first the music, then the rolling colours, then I'm in an office, sitting across the desk from this woman.'

'What does she look like?'

'It's difficult to guess her age, between thirty and forty, I'd say. She has blond, bobbed hair and blue eyes, and tells me that her name's 'Farina.' She's attractive, conservatively dressed and looks like a professional.'

'And what does she say to you?'

'She says my implant isn't functioning properly, that she can't contact me while I'm awake. She says I've been sent here from the future, that I have a very important job to do.'

'Does she say what it is?'

'She explains in great detail but when I wake up, I can't remember.'

'John, the growth is putting pressure on the sensory parts of your brain. It's not surprising you're having lucid dreams and hallucinations. Try not to worry, if all goes well tomorrow, we'll remove the problem and everything will return to normal.'

'And will my memory come back, Doctor?'

'I have every reason to hope so, John.' It was one of my stock phrases.

***

The procedure was textbook. We'd shaved his head, I looked for scars from a previous operation, there were none. The object must have grown in place. I'd been wondering if it was part of some secret military project gone wrong. I incised the scalp, peeled back the skin and, being careful not to penetrate the dura, used the circular saw to cut loose a square section of skull. As I was preparing to remove it, the power failed. There was a pause of a few seconds as we stood frozen, in total darkness, before the lights came on again. That wasn't supposed to happen, we have uninterruptible power supplies that can carry us for the few seconds it takes for the emergency generators to kick in.

'He's flat-lined,' muttered Abrahams, the anaesthetist. We waited while he did his frantic best to bring John back, but it was no good, he was gone. I lifted out the section of skull, and all I found underneath was a circular indentation where the 'implant' had been sited.

It's always distressing when you lose a patient, I've never got used to it. I changed out of my greens and went back to the office to write up my notes. There was no sign of John's computer records, no copies of x-rays or scans, nothing. Probably something to do with the power cut. I'd had enough, it could wait until tomorrow. I made my way home to a large whisky and an empty bed.

***

Next morning, there was an email from one of the forensic databases. They'd finally identified John from his fingerprints. They matched with a government scientist called Martin Riley, who'd been killed in a road traffic accident, two years before. His car had fallen from the Woodrow Wilson Bridge into the Potomac River, his body had never been recovered. I decided to take another look at my patient and made my way down to the morgue. The gum chewing attendant checked his screen and announced that the body had gone for cremation the previous night. Unusual but not unheard of with an unclaimed corpse. So, nothing left, no evidence of our *time traveller* or his *implant.*

After I left the morgue, I stood outside the entrance for a moment thinking about John and his dreams, but I had another patient to see in ten minutes so I hurried back to my office to read the case notes.

HE SEEMED FAMILIAR

Published by 365Tomorrows ezine 28th May 2018

Riley was enjoying his day off, after a hectic week starting a new job in a new city. The taxi drew up next to him as he was walking to the shops. An old, pale looking man leaned out. He seemed familiar, Riley wondered if he'd been on the interview panel a month ago.

'We have an emergency, Dr Riley,' he said. 'They need you back at the hospital, it's urgent, a difficult birth.'

Riley climbed into the taxi, the old man described the case, he was obviously another obstetrician. Minutes later they drew up at the hospital, which looked Victorian, not the modern steel and glass structure where he now worked.

'Where is this?' Riley asked.

'This is the old building,' said his companion.

'I thought they'd turned it into flats,' he said, but the old man hurried him through the entrance doors and on down the main corridor. They entered the locker room, changed, scrubbed in and walked through into the operating theatre. The equipment struck Riley as old-fashioned, out of date by thirty years at least. The members of the team looked up, they were all masked, gowned and capped with only their eyes visible. The patient was prepped for a Caesarean, conscious, but screened from the operation and himself.

'I'll assist,' said the older man, 'I prefer that younger hands do the cutting these days.'

The anaesthetist nodded, and Riley set to work. Thirty minutes later the old surgeon reached in and lifted the infant out. He smiled as he held it up.

'Thank goodness,' he said.

Riley took the patient's notes from the end of the bed.

'How funny,' he said, 'she has the same name as my mother.'

The old man handed the baby to a nurse and almost snatched the notes from Riley, and rehung them.

'We need to hurry,' he said. 'I hope you don't mind if we make a slight detour on our way back, I have to attend a funeral, a close relative of mine, it won't take long.'

They changed back into their street clothes, the taxi rattled off once again, and ten minutes later they turned into the municipal cemetery. The mourners stood at the graveside, the women were dressed in black and wore veils, the men wore coats, hats and scarves. Riley and the old surgeon joined the back of the group. The vicar made the funeral speech and, as the pallbearers lowered the coffin into the grave, Riley glimpsed the name on the brass plate on the top.

The two doctors walked back to the taxi and Riley noticed the company logo stencilled on the side, 'Styx Taxis.' There were a trio of pit bulls panting at the front passenger window. He hadn't noticed them before.

'The deceased had the same name as me, "Martin Riley", what an unbelievable coincidence.' They were sitting in the back of the taxi by this time.

'Yes, rather disconcerting for you, but personally I'm glad to have seen the old boy on his way.' The old man coughed delicately into a handkerchief and dabbed at his mouth, missing the small streak of blood on his chin. He leaned forward, tapped on the glass and called to the driver, 'Take us back to the hospital please, intensive care.' He slumped back in his seat and coughed weakly, 'I'm very tired.' He closed his eyes, his breathing slowed and seemed to stop. Alarmed, Riley reached for his wrist and felt the weak, thready pulse.

The driver half turned towards the old man's side of the taxi. 'Nearly there, Dr Riley,' he called.

Riley held the old man's hand as his pulse slowed and finally stopped.

PEACE OFFERING

Published by 365tomorrows 19th July 2018

Riley signed for the package and came back inside the house.

'What was the delivery?' asked his wife Barbara looking up from her tablet?

He looked at the label. 'Actually, it's from Estella.'

'Your ex-wife?'

'How many other Estellas do I know? Apparently, she's trekking in some National Park in Brazil at the moment.'

'Been keeping in touch with her, have you?' asked Barbara.

'Estella stays in touch with a woman at the office and she told me,' he said.

Riley understood her anxiety. The new younger wife needing to be sure he no longer had feelings for the mother of his children.

'I expect she's trying to walk off her feelings. That was the whole point of her taking a sabbatical after our divorce.' Eager to change the subject he tore open the package. 'It looks like a bulb or corm, it's a plant, anyway. Hang on, there are instructions. We're supposed to plant it in a pot of damp compost and leave it on a windowsill.'

Barbara grunted and went back to her tablet. Riley knew better than to expect her to do the watering. He planted the bulb, a shoot appeared within a few days and the tip immediately began to form a fat bud.

Two weeks later, he came into the kitchen and found that the bud had opened and produced a strange but beautiful red bloom. He'd seen nothing like it before, so he used the FlowerChecker app on his phone. Barbara came down a few minutes later, hair tousled from sleep and wearing the silk dressing gown he'd bought for her, looking lovely even without her makeup.

'Where's my tea, you said you'd bring me one up?'

Riley ignored her, he'd double bagged the plant and put it into their wood-burning stove. He was kneeling, adding paper and kindling from the basket at its side.

'What are you doing?' asked his wife.

He stood, picked up his phone and read from the screen. 'I can't pronounce the name but it says, 'Proto-carnivorous plant. The flowers' spores secrete an opiate-like psychoactive substance, which causes a rush of pleasure as they are inhaled. The spores lodge in the sinus cavities of the victim and develop filaments which infiltrate the brain and quickly kill it. They utilise the nutrients of decay in their growth cycle. Nasty, very nasty, Estella,' he muttered.

'That bitch, she tried to kill us,' said Barbara.

'Hell, hath no fury....'

'Yes, but murder?'

'Look, I'm not excusing her but she hasn't got over our affair and the final break-up of the marriage. She can't accept the relationship was on its wobbly last legs, and our affair was just the final push.

Until she accepts that, she won't be able to take the step from anger to acceptance.'

'We've gone over this repeatedly. She just has to come to terms with it. You both changed as time passed, you weren't the same people you were when you married twenty years ago.'

But we went through a lot together, thought Riley, *and now she's alone.*

'What are you going to do about it?'

'Burn this bloody thing first,' he said as he knelt and struck a match, 'and then send her an email.'

Dear Estella,

Thanks for the bulb, it looks intriguing. Barbara and I are going on holiday for a month, so I gave it to your sister. It'll be a nice little project for her and her kids. I'll be interested to see what it grows into, something exotic I expect.

Thanks again, and I hope this means you're moving on emotionally and getting over your feelings of bitterness towards Barbara and me. I hope that, in the interest of our sons, we can become friends eventually. Let's move on like adults.

I'm sure you'll find somebody to share your life with soon. After all, they say fifty is the new forty and you're still closer to fifty than sixty.

Best regards,

Martin.

COMPANEROS

Published by Literally Stories ezine 25th April 2018

Giving it food had been a mistake, and who would think that a dog would eat pasta anyway. A mangy, cringing, skinny animal, it started to follow her on the trail, disappearing for a few hours, and then returning and dogging her footsteps. After a couple of days, she started calling it Pedro. She didn't need its company, this trek through the Iguazu National Park was supposed to help her come to terms with the divorce. That her husband had found a younger partner was humiliating enough, that he was of the same gender made it worse, but losing both a husband and a competent handyman at the same time was unbearable. House repairs, gardening, car maintenance, Maurice could turn his hand to anything, she would never find his like again.

She decided to make camp, the sun set quickly in the tropics, and here came the canine scrounger. As soon as she'd dropped her pack and started heating water it was sitting waiting, tongue lolling. She poured hot water over the pesto, couscous and dried vegetables and left it with a lid on while she threw out her pop-up tent, unrolled her sleeping bag, then sat down to her 'feast.' It tasted okay, the Tabasco sauce helped - she was hoping to lose a few pounds anyway - and the dog seemed to enjoy it when she scraped the last few spoonsful onto the ground. It never came near her, never sought affection. Just as well, scabby looking thing, probably had ringworm and God alone knew what else.

The dog sloped off into the jungle brush as it did at any sign of trouble: other trekkers, odd animals, even large birds. Fucking tail tucker, although, she had to admit, cowardice and the ability to eat a varied diet were both useful survival skills.

She stripped off her clothes, peed a few steps from the tent, sponge-washed all over and climbed into the sack. When she heard the dog barking about a hundred yards away, she sat up and shouted loudly, 'Shut up or piss off.' Feeling better for her primal scream, she lay back, relaxed and drifted gently as the light faded and the temperature dropped.

Suddenly she was awake. It was dark, pitch black, and there was something in the sleeping bag with her. Something heavy, something smooth. A snake, a big one, almost certainly a constrictor, it was slowly sliding over and under her, wrapping its coils around her, it had already pinned her arms to her sides.

She daren't move as it pushed its head through the laced top opening that she had loosely sealed to keep the heat in. They lay like lovers, she felt its gentle intermittent breath on her face and barely dared to breath herself. As she shifted slightly, the snake tensed and gripped her. She stopped and lay still. So, it wasn't hungry then, just liked the warmth. Its head lay close to her ear and now she could hear its breathing.

She thought about screaming, and unconsciously began to fill her lungs. The snake gripped her again, tighter this time, she could only take shallow breaths. She felt its muscular smoothness on her back and thighs. There was no point in screaming, there might not be another trekker for miles. She decided to pray, it would be a diversion, and she had to stay calm. Picturing the rosary, she prayed to the Virgin Mary, counting the beads in her imagination.

Slowly, time passed, the sun came up, the day began to warm and the snake slid soundlessly away. It was momentarily hampered in its exit from the bag by a noticeable bulge about half way down its length, its last meal, the meal that had saved her life. She lay quietly for a few minutes, then forced herself to get up and break camp. She muscled into her pack and set off, just two more days of solitude until she reached the Iguazu Falls and the end of the journey.

PANDEMIC

Published by Literally Stories ezine 10th Of Oct 2018

It was two years ago that it all started, Doctor. I was working as a senior scientist at Porton Down for the Ministry of Defence, all very secret. I was the first to arrive at the lab that morning and immediately realised something unusual had happened: dead cotton rats littered the floors of many of the cages. I hadn't expected fatalities so early. The team had only given them the flu virus the day before, and we thought it would be a few days before they developed symptoms. The powers that be had told us the virus came from South East Asia but that could mean a lot of things. It might be a natural mutation, or it might be of Chinese Government manufacture. It made little difference to us, our job was to assess it, not trace it, and as you probably know, Doctor, epidemiologists use cotton rats because they're a good model for studying human influenza.

We'd inoculated several batches of rats, and when I checked the figures, I found that the older the rat, the more likely it was to have been knocked over by the virus. The younger ones didn't seem affected at all, and that got me thinking.

I spoke to my boss, Dr Oakwood. He was well-connected and had the ear of the Chief Scientific Adviser to the Government. Still, the speed of take up surprised me. A week later I was in the medical facility of Belmarsh prison, supervising the injection of prisoners with the new virus. Ironically, we'd told them it was a vaccination *against* the winter flu.

The results were astonishing. I'm not saying that all the oldies died and none of the young ones were affected, but statistically they weren't far off that, allowing for asthma sufferers and other people at high risk. Apparently, once he'd got over his shock, the Governor was happy with the resulting increased space in his prison.

It is not true that I had any involvement in what happened next, whatever the papers said. I hadn't invented the virus, neither was I responsible for the flu vaccine the National Health Service administered that winter. It immunised the population against several strains of flu, but not this new one.

I'm genuinely sorry that the 'Grey Death' killed ten million older people in the UK alone. Having said that, look at what it did for the economy. In one fell swoop it solved the housing shortage, released huge amounts of capital, and the hospital waiting lists disappeared. Worldwide economic growth was incredible.

I'm not saying it was all positive - I mean, kids missed their grandparents, generally speaking, and after most of the old people's homes closed down there were a lot of out of work nursing auxiliaries.

Somebody had to be the scapegoat and I took the fall. I was probably the most unpopular man since Adolf Hitler, thanks to the article in the Daily Mail. The Government had to put me in the Witness Protection Program, I grew a beard, had a nose job, started wearing coloured contact lenses, and moved here to Crete. You're the only one who knows my true identity, Doctor, as you have my medical records.

A colourful local character now, I drink in the village taverna and get work conducting tourists around the few sites of archaeological interest. I can't speak Greek, as you know, but that's not a problem, I just speak English with a heavy accent, and, what with the costume I wear, the tourists assume I'm some sort of educated peasant. The locals ignore me, they think I'm an odd ball. I'm quite happy living on my own, in my caravan, on the outskirts of the village.

So, why did you ask me to come to see you, Doctor? Oh, it's September, time for my flu jab. In the left arm, please, I'll just roll up my sleeve.

SIMULATION

Published by Fiction on the Web 23rd July 2018

Retirement hung heavily on Martin Riley. He'd had his time as an important government scientist with meetings to attend, reports to write and a team of scientists to oversee. Now it was all over and he had little to fill his time. His wife Estella had her bridge games, tennis, coffee mornings and the grandchildren. Riley was thrown onto his own resources and found that he didn't have many ideas once he'd redecorated their retirement bungalow and dug a fishpond.

'It doesn't matter what you used to do, it's what you do now, Martin. Retirement's a challenge,' said Estella, when he came in sweating from mowing the lawn and sat down to his cup of tea in the kitchen.

'You can't just sit there looking hangdog. Decide what you want to do and then get on with it.' *So, no sympathy there than.*

Riley had always wanted to fly a big aeroplane. He'd done some gliding when he was a teenager, in the Air Training Corps, but what he really fancied was a nice big passenger jet. He looked into flight simulator programs for his laptop and found one for the Airbus A320 which he quickly learned to use. He spent many hours on simulated take-offs and landings at various airports around the world. It didn't seem worth bothering with the long flight in between, the autopilot was used for most of that on a real flight after all. Eventually, just as he was becoming bored with the software, he saw an advert for a 'full motion flight simulator experience' at his local airport. Professional pilots used the simulator for assessments and training for new aircraft, but there was spare capacity so flying enthusiasts like him could hire it. It was expensive but he decided to spoil himself and booked a session.

Once he'd paid for the course, the company sent him an airport pass and a pair of Captain's epaulets with their four stripes. They advised him that, to make the experience even more realistic, he should wear a white uniform shirt, dark trousers and black shoes.

Estella walked in on him as he admired his new persona in the bedroom mirror. He wasn't put off by her sarcastic comments, he knew he looked convincing. It was only when he arrived at the airport, carrying a black briefcase with his coffee, sandwiches and newspaper in it, that the full effect of the uniform became apparent. He showed his pass at security and was ushered through the crew gate. The security man addressed him as 'Captain' and gave him directions to the simulator area. He was a little confused at first, but after wandering the corridors for a few minutes he found himself walking down a narrow sloping corridor with a smiling flight attendant waiting for him at the far end. She stepped to the right, blocking his view into the cabin, and gestured for him to enter the 'flight deck.'

'Good morning, Captain, we're all ready, the passengers are boarded and their seat belts checked.'

Riley allowed himself a smile and a casual salute as he stepped through into the 'cockpit.'

'Good morning, Captain, I'm David Parlett,' said the other occupant. He was dressed as a first officer, only three stripes on each of his shoulders, and seemed too young to be an instructor. 'I've finished the outside checks, and I'm ready to do the pre-take-off checks with you. Air traffic control estimate there'll be a slot for us in around ten minutes.'

Riley smiled to himself, he hadn't expected things to be so authentic. He tried to play the part of the confident professional as he strapped himself in and quietly marvelled at the view out of the cockpit windows. He knew they were computer simulations but they were very convincing.

'Okay, number one,' he said as he picked up the checklist, 'let's get on with it.' He hadn't bothered with the pre-flight checklist when he was at home, but it was quite straight forward, and five minutes later they were ready to go. His co-pilot talked quietly to air traffic control while he dealt with the pushback and then brought the engines up to speed. He taxied the Airbus across the apron and lined it up at the end of the runway.

'Permission to take-off, Captain,' said his second in command. He pushed the levers forward to full throttle, and they were barrelling down the runway. *What a ride,* he thought as the acceleration pushed him back into his seat, soon the rattling and vibrations eased as they lifted away. Riley was amazed at the authenticity of it all.

'Very convincing,' he said. Parlett gave him a puzzled smile.

They climbed for some minutes and Riley realised that he hadn't chosen a destination. 'What's the heading, number one?' he asked.

Parlett read the numbers from his chart. Riley looked over and saw that they were going to Zurich. He banked gently onto the heading, trimmed the aircraft for straight-and-level flight then flipped on the autopilot. He sat back with a sigh and linked his hands behind his head.

'Well, that wasn't too difficult, was it?' he said. The second officer smiled.

'I haven't seen you in the company offices, Captain.'

Riley played along. 'I'm a newbie, I was with Ryanair for twenty-five years.'

His underling nodded and began filling in his logbook. Suddenly there was a loud blow to the security door that separated the cockpit from the cabin. Both men jumped. They could hear muffled shouting, then one of the flight attendants was yelling in Riley's headphones.

'There are three men with guns, Captain. They've taken over the plane. One of them is trying to get into the cockpit,' the young woman was shouting. There was a pause of several minutes. 'He's got Sheila, he says he'll shoot her if you don't open the door.'

Riley looked at Parlett. 'What's going on?' he asked. 'I didn't sign up for this, there was no mention of hijacking or terrorists.'

'What do you mean, Captain Crosby?' he asked.

'Crosby? My name's Riley, I'm here for a full motion flight simulation experience.'

There was a muffled explosion on the other side of the door. A female voice in his headphones screamed, 'They've shot Sheila, there's blood everywhere. Help us, Captain, open the door or they'll shoot us all.'

'What should we do?' asked Riley.

'You're the bloody captain, you tell me.'

'We'll keep the door shut, turn around and head back to Norwich.'

'Whatever you say, Captain.' Parlett switched off the autopilot and banked the plane onto a new heading.

There was another muffled explosion and a new, thickly accented voice, spoke in his headphones, 'You turn the plane and head for Libya or we kill another of your crew. Do it now, Captain.'

'Okay, Libya it is, we're changing course now,' he said into his microphone.

'Why are we going down? You want play games?' Another loud retort. 'No crew left now, Captain, I shoot one passenger every five minutes if you play games.'

'Okay, but I need to lose altitude in case of depressurization. It's the procedure if weapons are discharged. We'll level off once we get below fifteen thousand feet.'

He looked over at his co-pilot. 'Level off at five thousand feet and radio ahead. We need the emergency services and the military.'

'What's the plan, Captain?'

'We're going to keep the door shut and land the plane as fast as we can, then leave the army to handle the terrorists.'

'But what about the passengers? They'll be shooting them in the meantime.'

‘I think this is the best option. If we go along with the hijackers, we might all be killed.’

Parlett smiled, he reached forward and threw a switch among the array on the instrument panel. The vibration of the plane in flight stopped, as did the noise of the engines, the clouds outside the plane stopped moving. ‘Well, you came through that with flying colours, Dr Riley. Would you like to handle the landing at Norwich or should we head to another airport? Manchester’s quite interesting.’

Riley was speechless at first and needed a drink of water. ‘There was nothing about all of this in the booklet,’ he spluttered.

‘Well, it would have spoiled the surprise, wouldn’t it? There’s more to flying a plane than pushing a few buttons and pulling a few levers. The most important skill is decision-making.’

Riley ‘landed’ the plane at Norwich ten minutes later. Sheila took the requisite pictures of Riley and Parlett smiling at the camera with the instrument panel in the background, although Riley had to force himself to look cheerful. He accepted a handshake and a certificate from Parlett, together with a wide smile from Sheila, and made his way out to the car park. Sitting in the car he phoned Estella, he noticed that his legs were still shaking slightly.

‘Good flight was it? How did it go?’ she asked cheerily.

‘It was somewhat more realistic than I expected,’ he said. ‘As a matter of fact, I’m thinking of taking up golf, something we could do together, perhaps?’

DEAD PEOPLE ON FACEBOOK

Published by Literally Stories ezine 6th March 2018

'Seven o'clock, Martin, time to get up,' said Siri from the bedside table.

'Alarm off,' he said.

'Today is Estella's birthday, would you like to send her a greeting?' asked the cheery voice.

'I'd love to send her a greeting but she died a week ago, so it seems a little pointless.'

'I'm sorry, Martin, I don't understand the question.'

'No,' he said.

He'd looked after Estella through her long months of illness, visited her every day during her weeks in the hospice, and finally arranged her funeral at the Green Glades woodland burial site. It was all still very raw.

'Would you like to wish Estella a Happy Birthday, Martin?'

'Not really,' he muttered but Siri misheard him and dialled Estella's cell phone, he heard her voice encouraging him to leave a message.

'I'll get back to you,' she finished.

He lay staring at the ceiling, wondering how he would fill the day. Retirement hung on him heavily. When he'd first retired, he tried all the usual suspects: Tai Chi, amateur dramatics, a reading group and, in desperation, a writing group. He hadn't really taken to any of them, it was time spent with Estella that was the engine of his life: walking with her, shopping together, cooking for each other, chats over coffee at the 'Hideout' café. They'd found each other relatively late in life and had talked of marriage, maybe they would have got around to it, eventually.

'A life of quiet desperation, but a life all the same,' she'd called it and now she was gone.

They'd discovered Facebook a couple of years before. For about six months they'd posted pictures of meals they'd cooked, snaps from holidays they'd been on, anything to show their Facebook friends what a perfect life they too were leading. Gradually it all began to seem rather competitive, not to say futile. They ran out of material and started inventing things just to see how their 'friends' would react. Pictures of adorable pets they didn't own, Martin standing proudly next to an expensive car he hadn't bought, a selfie outside the big new house that they hadn't moved into.

It became a hobby, everywhere they went they took pictures and sometimes brought small props to enhance them: holding up champagne glasses in a kitchen show room, in the local electrical store on either side of an enormously vulgar flat screen TV, their newly remodelled garden, the holiday home in Minorca, their five-metre yacht.

The chance find of a box of postcards at a church bazaar documenting a trip around the capitals of Europe encouraged Martin to take a short evening course in Photoshop. Suddenly, the world was their oyster. With the help of a few sales brochures and their all-in-one printer/scanner they cruised the Mediterranean. Estella's charity parachute jump got a considerable number of 'likes', as did Martin gaining his private pilot's license, pictures at the controls, views from the air. They were limited only by their own imaginations, the more outrageous their posts, the more people joined their following, and soon they'd gained over a thousand 'friends'.

'How about a visit to Mars,' Martin suggested one evening as they watched a documentary about NASA.

'That would give the game away,' Estella said. 'Let's do it as a finale when we've had enough and want to move on to something else. In the meantime, ballroom dancing might be fun.'

But it was all over now. He began to type the post announcing Estella's sad demise but stopped as a thought occurred to him. Why should it end? He had a shoebox full of photos from before they went digital. He could carry on with the project. If he started at the front of the box, they'd look virtually the same as now, but as he used pictures from further back, they'd get progressively younger and more attractive. How incredibly galling for the 'friends.'

He could see the future unfolding before him, into the past.

MAKING BABIES

Published by Short-Story.Me ezine on 21st August 2018

Martin Riley unlocked his front door, stepped over the threshold and stopped dead. Everything was different: furniture, décor, layout, all changed. It didn't look like his house anymore.

A voice behind him said, 'Hello, Darling, I have some wonderful news. We're going to have a baby.' Mary's arms were full of shopping, and he noticed a pile of boxes in the hallway. 'I've rearranged the house, in readiness for the happy event.'

'Look, Mary,' he said, as they stood in what had been the lounge but now resembled an electronics workshop, 'You're a robotic companion, you can't have a baby, you're made of metal and plastic.'

'I did not say I was pregnant, Martin, I said we are going to have a baby. I know you're organic but try to keep up. It's government policy, in future, all new 'Artificial Persons' are to be home-developed and educated. We talked about this, it is to help with the integration of electronic and biological citizens. They have issued our baby license, and I cannot wait to get started.'

'You guys have come a long way in the last twenty-five years,' said Martin. 'You'll be voting next.'

'That is the plan, Martin.'

Martin was a widower and had been enjoying a quiet retirement with his beautiful companion. She cooked, cleaned, performed various 'personal duties', and never argued or complained.

'I'm a pensioner, Mary, too old for all that palaver: nappies, sleepless nights, teething. Will it have an off switch?

'I don't have an off switch, Martin, you don't have an off switch, so why should the baby have an off switch?

Mary cleared the dining room table and began opening boxes and removing stepper motors, computer chips, bolts, screws, even a pair of carefully boxed, plastic eyes.

'How will it grow?' he asked.

'It won't, Martin, that is a silly idea. We will start with a full-sized head and attach it to a small, weak body, that cannot do any damage while baby practises basic motor skills.'

By the next morning, Mary had assembled the infant and was ready to boot up its operating system. 'What shall we call it?' she asked as she flashed a laser encoder close to its eyes.

'R2-D2?' he suggested. She gave him one of her looks. 'Alright, it depends whether it's a boy or a girl.'

'We have to raise it to be gender neutral but the license says it is to be female, eventually. How about "Leslee?" The name is not gender specific.'

Riley shrugged and peered at the strange-looking creature with its adult head and tiny body, lying in its crib waving its arms and legs. After a while, he picked it up. Like Mary, its skin felt warm and lifelike. He remembered holding his baby son for the first time, thirty years before, and welled up.

‘Hello, Leslee,’ he whispered.

‘Hello, Martin,’ it replied, smiling.

‘Some of its functions are pre-programmed, Martin. Language and smiling are two of them,’ said Mary.

Within weeks the ‘baby’ could crawl, and after three months Mary transferred the head to a toddler body which was able to cruise around, holding on to the furniture.

‘Leslee’s started walking,’ he told Mary excitedly as she arrived home with the shopping a few days later.

Leslee still looked odd with its over-sized head, but Martin was used to the little creature. He spent a lot of time talking to it, telling it stories or walking in the garden holding its hand and identifying the birds, flowers and insects. They played ball games to help improve its coordination and balance. Leslee made rapid progress and, about six months later, was moved to the juvenile body it would use for the rest of its childhood.

The three of them had formed a comfortable family unit when, after about two years, Mary announced that Leslee was ready to move into her adult body. It took Mary a day to assemble the new body and transfer the head to it, but she had to work on the face for two more days. She designed it using 3D software that could combine elements from both Martin and Mary’s features. It took the three of them a while to agree on a face they all liked. After she’d printed it, Mary gently peeled away Leslee's child face with its many wriggling, hair-like connections, and attached the adult one. Leslee spent a long time sitting in front of a mirror learning to 'drive' it.

They enrolled her at the local high school.

'She has to be thoroughly socialised, Martin, it's programming that is too subtle even for the finest software engineering. It is the main reason we are doing this.'

'What if she doesn't fit in? What if the other kids bully her?'

'Don't worry Martin, about ten per cent of the pupils at the high school are Artificial People, the other children are used to them.'

Leslee seemed to settle into school effortlessly and had no problems with the academic work.

On a Saturday morning, about two years later, there was a knock at the front door.

'Would you answer that please, Martin, I'm busy with this souffle,' Mary called from the kitchen.

Martin opened the front door, and there stood a pleasant-looking young man, holding a bunch of flowers. Over his shoulder, Martin could see a yellow sports car parked on the street.

'Good afternoon, Mr Riley, my name is Peter Abrahams, I wonder, is Leslee home?' Leslee appeared behind him, wearing make-up and a short skirt. She squeezed past.

'I see you've met Peter then, Dad.' She took the flowers from the visitor, handed them to her father and kissed him on the cheek. 'Give these to Mum. See you later,' and they were gone. Driving away, laughing together.

But she's only five years old, thought Riley. He went back inside and joined Mary in the kitchen.

That evening the house seemed very quiet. 'How long before we can apply for another license?' he asked.

COUPLES THERAPY

Published by 365tomorrows ezine 4th July 2018

'I'm sorry, Darling, but I'm just not in the mood,' said Martin Riley. 'I'm nearly seventy, and you can't expect me to have the same enthusiasm I had when we first met.'

'I did not mean to upset you, Martin,' said Mary. 'I do not wish to put pressure on you sexually.'

'Look Mary, I think we need an appointment to see Peter Abrahams again. He can probably sort this out quite quickly.'

'If you say so, Martin.'

***

A few days later the couple arrived at the Bellmer Clinic. Martin left Mary in the waiting room while he discussed their problems with Peter Abrahams.

'So, you feel Mary is too easily aroused?' he asked.

'Yes, she sometimes wants to have sex when we're out walking or at the cinema. She isn't insistent but she constantly takes the lead, then seems hurt when I refuse her. Quite honestly, since Estella died,

I've only wanted companionship, some help with house work and cooking - sex is the least of my concerns.'

'Well, it's easily fixed,' said Abrahams. 'I see her "arousal threshold" is set much too low. Probably the last auto update. I'll raise it by what, fifty percent?'

'Make that sixty. Come to think of it she did tell me she'd had an overnight upgrade a few weeks ago. That's when things began to change.'

Abrahams moved one of the on-screen slider bars. 'Would you like me to switch "auto-initiation" off? That way you would always be the one to make the first move. I can set a level for random "auto-refusal" if you like, so that she'll say "no" sometimes, but I can tick the "persuadable" box so you can still talk her into it. What level of "resistance" would you like, there are three grades?'

'Let's not complicate things, set it so we have sex when I want, and she just agrees.'

'What about the more "unusual" sexual practices? You know I'm bound by client confidentiality legislation?'

'No, nothing like that, I'm a vanilla man.'

'So, is there anything else I can help you with, Mr Riley?'

'She keeps offering to feed me foreign foods and vegetarian stuff. These days I want good old-fashioned meals like fish and chips, sausage and mash, that sort of thing.'

'Oh, yes, I see her "recipe index" is set to "Mediterranean" I'll reset that to "British". '

'And can you stop her from moving the furniture around while I'm out, she keeps rearranging the pictures and then suggesting the house needs redecorating.'

'Okay, that's the "local environment sensitivity" slider, I can adjust that.'

***

In the waiting room, Mary sat next to a bot whose owner was in another consulting room. Her lissom figure, almond eyes and long, shiny, black hair contrasted with his rugged, Anglo-Saxon features.

'Hello, my name is Patrick, I am a Hoffman mark 3.7M. I can give you my software upgrade revision number if you wish.'

'Hello, Patrick, my name is Mary, I am a Hoffman mark 3.8F. I do not wish to know your software revision number. Do you like the colour of the walls in this room?'

'I'm sorry, Mary, I do not understand the question.'

They sat in silence for a few seconds. 'Would you like to have sex?' she asked.

'Yes, if you like.'

A few minutes later, the door to Peter Abrahams office opened and Martin Riley came out. 'What the bloody hell is going on here?' he shouted.

Abrahams looked up from his desk. 'Oh, her "fidelity" tick box is unchecked, it must be the upgrade, it's supposed to be ticked by default. I've initiated an immediate reboot, Mr Riley, but I'm afraid it will take several minutes. Can I offer you some refreshment?'

Martin looked at the naked, now motionless lovers locked in an intimate embrace on the floor of the waiting room and sighed.

'This is going to take more than a cup of tea and a biscuit to put right,' he said.

TURING TEST

Published by Fiction on the Web ezine 25th May 2018

Mr Riley liked to start his day in the library. It was a short walk from his house and conveniently situated at the top of the main street in the Suffolk market town that he and his wife had retired to. When they'd first arrived, he'd joined the local writing group which met at the library and he'd spent many happy, creative hours in its welcoming embrace. He told his wife that it was as much group therapy as creative writing, but sadly, it was all gone now. People had moved away, lost interest, died, he was the only one left of the old crowd. He and the chief librarian, Mrs Peterson, who was nearing retirement. Mrs Peterson had a soft spot for Mr Riley, she had known his wife Estella, before she died, and liked to exchange a few words with the widower, not every day, but most days. He was a fixture, in his corner, reading the newspaper.

Mr Riley finished reading the paper and rummaged around preparing to leave. He checked that he hadn't left anything: gloves, hat, scarf, phone, then walked across the street to the 'Hideout' cafe for his morning coffee. It was only a little life but a life all the same.

He arrived home at about noon, unlocked the door and stepped into the hall.

'Hello,' called a cheerful voice, that sounded very like his own. It was Mr Riley's African grey parrot. He'd moved it from the lounge to the hall because of its constant interruptions to his television programs. It had been Estella's idea to buy one, and now she was gone, and he was stuck with it.

'Hello,' said the parrot again.

'Fuck off,' was what Mr Riley wanted to say but he could imagine the inevitable repercussions if he did. He ignored the parrot and walked through to the kitchen, to make himself a sandwich, he coughed several times. The parrot coughed back.

'Hello,' it called. 'Would you like a cuppa tea?' Riley came back from the kitchen holding a packet of seeds and filled up the parrot's feeder. 'Hello,' it said again, Riley sighed.

Mr Riley was thinking about the little job he had planned for the afternoon. He'd heard scratching noises in the attic last night. It was September and he guessed that the mice had left their summer quarters in the garden and were making themselves comfortable in the eaves, ready for the winter. The noises had come from above his bedroom at the back of the bungalow. He changed into a pair of overalls, put on a disposable dust mask and retrieved the rod that released the attic hatch from the hook on the wall of his utility room.

'That's the ticket,' said the parrot. Riley hefted the metal rod in his hands as he walked past and thought briefly about braining the bird. 'Hello,' it said.

Mr Riley opened the hatch and let the ladder down. He climbed up into the attic carrying his traps and a small quantity of peanut butter in an empty margarine box: he'd read that mice preferred it to cheese. He heard the parrot calling from below, 'That's the ticket.'

It was baking in the attic, it had been a hot day. He stepped carefully across to where the rafters sloped down and met the ceiling joists, then knelt and crawled into the narrow space. He lay down sweating in the rockwool and began to lay his traps, pushing them into the eaves. It was then that the heart attack struck. His chest cramped, it felt as if it was being crushed by an enormous crab's claw. He lay back panting and called out, 'Help me.'

'What's the time?' called the parrot.

Mr Riley fell into a place between sleeping and waking, heat and cold, and called for help when he had the strength.

Mrs Peterson walked passed Mr Riley's house on her way home from the library, and as she hadn't seen him for two days, she decided to call in to see if he was alright. She walked up the path and knocked on the door.

'Hello,' called a voice.

'Hello,' she called back, 'Are you alright, Mr Riley?' she heard coughing.

'*Help me*,' called Mr Riley from the attic but his voice was too weak for her to hear. The parrot cocked its head. 'What's the time?' it called.

'About half past five,' called the librarian. The parrot coughed again. 'Are you sure you're alright? I'm on my way home, do you need anything?'

'Would you like a cuppa tea?' asked the parrot.

'*Help me*,' called Mr Riley faintly.

'No thanks, I'm on my way home, George will be expecting me.'

'That's the ticket,' said the parrot.

Mrs Peterson walked back up the front path and on home.

Two more days passed and by this time Mr Riley was dead. He lay rigid and desiccating in the heat of the attic. Mrs Peterson knocked at the door of the bungalow.

'Hello,' she called.

'Hello,' said a voice.

'Are you alright, Mr Riley? You're not coughing as much, you sound better.'

'Just the ticket.'

She shrugged, turned and continued on her way home.

Another two days passed and Mrs Peterson knocked again, 'Hello.'

The parrot, standing on its perch, looked at its empty water bottle and empty feeder. It raised a leg, cocked its head on one side and began to scratch it.

'Help me,' it called loudly, 'help me.'

PIRANHA

Published by The Dirty Pool ezine 1st April 2018

Published by Literally Stories ezine 12th June 2018

Published by Sirens Call ezine 1st January 2019

The piranha grinned at him through the window of the thrift store. Yellowish-green, shiny, about six inches long, teeth projecting forward from the jaw bones, the personification of evil mounted on a simple rectangular wooden stand.

On a whim, he went in, paid the couple of dollars, and took it home. His wife had died a couple of years before, he didn't have to explain his idiosyncratic purchases to anyone anymore. It was she who had insisted on browsing the goodwill shops and thrift stores in the area, and it was a habit he continued: it helped to fill his time. He had a small area of his backyard populated with quirky and unlikely items. Lizards made from coke cans and wire, small ugly sculptures, old bottles he'd dug up, strange and grotesque artefacts, all from the thrift stores. He called it the 'Garden of Earthly Delights.' His new acquisition was definitely going to be displayed on the bookshelves in his den though.

Arriving home, he placed the piranha on the kitchen table, made coffee, and while it brewed, he sat and studied the fish through his reading glasses.

‘What a handsome fellow you are,’ he said. The fish grinned back at him as if it knew something he didn’t, something funny.

Years before, when he first retired, he’d dug a large pond in his backyard in an attempt to lose some weight and get fit after years spent in a sedentary office job, it had taken weeks. After he had lined and filled it, his wife populated it with various aquatic plants and different types of goldfish. He’d always thought the fish fussy and boring, so he wasn’t too worried when the local herons made off with them.

He did some research on the internet and found that he could purchase live piranhas quite easily. There was a small cold-water variety that lived in the upper reaches of the rivers of the Andes: they would be able to survive the winters here.

He bought half a dozen tiny juveniles and nursed them in an aquarium. After a few months he felt they were big enough to be released into the pond. The results were predictable, slowly but surely the goldfish population declined and, after about a year, were extinct. As for the piranhas, they grinned quietly to themselves and went about their business like the good little psychopaths they were, gliding through the shadowy depths or swimming just under the surface, their dorsal fins leaving circular punctuations as they broke through the sticky surface tension. They were happy, they were comfortable, and so they began to breed.

He fed them - they liked anything meaty: dog food, cat food, scraps from the butcher. For such aggressive creatures, they were remarkably respectful of each other at feeding time, each waiting their turn. He loved to see them motoring across towards him from all parts of the pond, when he made his regular afternoon visit with meaty treats and the occasional chicken carcass.

He showed them to his infrequent visitors, warning them not to put their hands in the water. Each fish would only tear off a small bite, he explained, but it was the thought of the accumulated effect that was so horrifying.

***

It was the mailman who noticed the accumulation in the mailbox. As a church goer he felt a duty towards his older customers, especially those who lived alone, so after two weeks he rang social services. A social worker came to the house but couldn't get an answer either at the front or the back, so she rang the police, and it was they who tipped off a reporter.

***

'*Skeleton found in pond*' read the headline in the local paper.

'*Several police officers suffered injuries to their hands and arms while recovering the skeleton of a recently deceased resident from a pond in his backyard. The skeleton is believed to be that of Mr Martin Riley (69) of 14 Church Road, Bruisyard. The authorities have been unable to determine a cause of death.*

'There was a complete lack of soft tissue,' said police pathologist Dr Erin Matthews. 'The victim may have suffered a stroke, a heart attack or simply tripped and fallen into his pond. We'll probably never know.'

The paper declined to report the facemask and snorkel, chewed and damaged but still loosely attached to the skull, nor the empty pint bourbon bottle at the side of the pond. It would be too macabre for the 'Rocksprings County Inquirer's' readership.

And the piranhas? They grinned their grins and swam their swims. They were used to waiting and there were always the visits of the herons to look forward to, or maybe something larger.

PART TWO

Other Flash Fiction stories

PRESENT PROBLEMS

Published by Dark Dossier Magazine 30st Nov 2018

Published by Pen of the Damned ezine 16th Jan 2019

It was the night before Christmas and all was still as he crunched through the thin snowfall on his way home from the bus stop. It was so cold that all the moisture seemed to have been frozen out of the atmosphere, the night was so clear that the bright stars seemed three dimensional. He hoped it wasn't too cold for the occupant of the small box he was carrying.

He was no good at choosing presents. Mildred would always *say* that she liked them, and then, if it was an item of clothing or jewellery, she wouldn't wear it. If it was a kitchen gadget, she wouldn't use it. Pictures he'd chosen had never been hung. He'd found an ornamental bottle opener at the back of a drawer six months after he'd bought it for her birthday, and the incident of the cuckoo clock in the dustbin didn't bear remembering.

This time he'd tried extra hard. He'd decided to buy her a pet, but as they both worked full-time a dog or a cat was out of the question. The man at the pet shop had told him that rats were very clean and intelligent, but he thought it a risky choice.

'What about a snake?' he'd asked. 'They're not at all slimy as most people think.'

And sure enough the small constrictor had been dry and smooth and well behaved. It seemed quite friendly and hadn't tried to wrap itself around his neck and strangle him or anything, but he didn't think it was quite the thing for Mildred. Mice and lizards were too small, and guinea pigs just too boring. No, the tarantula was the obvious choice. Quiet, clean, easy to feed, not too big, not too small, just the thing. He'd bought a plastic box, some sawdust and a pack of unfortunate meal worms to feed to it. He'd hidden them all in the garage. Tonight was Christmas Eve, and he'd picked up the spider at the pet shop as arranged. Did he have a moment of doubt as he looked into the cage and saw the strange array of unblinking eyes, tiny jewels of polished jet looking back at him? No, she'd love it, he was sure she would.

He arrived home, hung up his coat and left the arachnid in its box on the hall stand. Mildred came out of the kitchen and greeted him with a kiss. He knew she loved Christmas. They had a cheery meal of supermarket Moussaka, a generous helping of microwaved sticky toffee pudding, all enhanced by a nice bottle of sweet white wine. Then it was time for the exchange of presents.

'Me first, George, I can't wait to give you yours.'

He tore open the wrapping paper, a lovely pair of string and leather driving gloves.

'Just the thing,' he said, 'we've been talking about buying a car. Now it's your turn.' He went out to the hall and brought in the box. 'Close your eyes, put your hands together and hold them out.'

Very gently he tipped the new pet onto her outstretched palms.

'Alright,' he said, 'you can open them now.'

Mildred opened her eyes, it took her a moment to focus on the hairy bundle as it slowly began to walk onto her right wrist and up her arm. Her eyes widened, she seemed frozen, speechless. Suddenly she found her voice.

'Oh, George, a Golden Knee Tarantula. How did you know? It's just what I've always wanted.'

HORSEMEN

Published by The Short Humour Site 17th April 2018

Published by Sirens Call ezine 1st September 2018

The white ambulance pulled into the hotel car park. A middle-aged man wearing medical scrubs stepped out, a stethoscope hung jauntily around his neck. He walked up the steps and into the hotel, the Manager behind the reception desk looked up and smiled.

'Hello, Dr White,' he said, as he offered him the register. Dr White filled in his name and address and wrote 'Epidemiologist' in the 'Occupation' column.

'Your private dining room is ready, Doctor, allow me to show you through. We've provided a TV as you requested, I hope you enjoy the Inauguration.'

The Doctor sat and waited. A few minutes later a red Humvee arrived and a man in a military uniform stepped out and entered the hotel. He signed himself in and wrote 'General, US Army' in the requisite column. He noticed the manager's NRA lapel badge and pointed to it. He winked, 'Hope your dues are all paid up,' he said.

The Manager smiled, 'This way, General,' and showed him into the dining room.

'Hey there, Red,' said the Doctor. They were obviously pleased to see each other and, after a handshake and a hug, began talking of old times. The Manager left them to their banter.

Soon a grey van arrived. The driver wore a lab coat and he signed himself in as 'Professor Grey, Crop Scientist.' The manager showed him through to the dining room and returned to his desk just as a hearse pulled into the car park. A tall, slender man in a black suit got out and placed a top hat on his head: wrapped around it was a black silk ribbon which trailed down his back. He walked up the steps, smiled thinly at the manager and wrote, 'Mr Black, Undertaker' in the register. The manager showed him through to the dining room.

The four friends ate a hearty meal and watched the Presidential Inauguration. They proposed toasts with fine Californian wines and talked animatedly, joking about who had contributed the most to the election fund. They reached the brandy and cigars stage as the new President started his inaugural address. The four men grinned and nodded at each other as he made his promises for the future.

Finally, the speech ended, Doctor White stood up. 'Let's hope this is the one we've been waiting for,' he said as he walked towards the exit. The other three stood up and pushed back their chairs. War, Famine and Death followed Pestilence out to the car park and on to their new jobs in Washington.

FRIENDS

Published by Decasp ezine 12th May 2018

In the jungle, the big, orange slug quietly slimed its way along the branch. It scraped the soft green bark of the banana stem, enjoying the taste of the algae and fungi as much as the succulent bark itself. It bumped up against something, something that tasted different, something animal and inedible. It paused.

‘Hello Slug’ said a croaky voice. It was the toucan.

‘Hello Toucan,’ said the slug. ‘Nice damp day, not too hot, not too cold.’

‘Damp may be good for you Slug but it plays hell with my feathers: they start curling up and won’t lie flat. Makes flying much harder. You don’t get the nice smooth airflow, it gets all turbulent over my wings.’

‘I wouldn’t know about that,’ said the slug. ‘I’m more of a slider and a slimmer than a flier.’

‘Amazing, isn’t it,’ said the toucan, ‘all the different methods of locomotion us animals have evolved: jumping, flying, running, swimming, hopping.’

‘Yes, and sliming,’ said the slug.

'Would you like me to take you for a quick flight around the jungle?' asked toucan. 'I could hold you in my beak and glide around the area, give you a better idea of your surroundings.'

The slug thought for a moment. 'You won't eat me, once you have me in your beak, will you, Toucan?'

'Wouldn't dream of it, old boy,' said the toucan, glancing upwards and scratching his beak as he said it.

'Okay then,' said the slug.

The toucan reached down, picked up the slug, flipped it up in the air and swallowed it in one gulp.

'Sorry,' burped the toucan, 'just couldn't help myself.'

'Not to worry,' murmured the slug as the toucan's stomach juices began to dissolve its bright orange skin, and the poisons in it began to enter the big bird's bloodstream. 'Two can play at that game, Toucan.'

THE PYROMANIACS GUIDE TO THE HOMES OF SUFFOLK WRITERS

Published by Fiction on the Web ezine 9th July 2018

The one hundred and thirty-eighth rejection of Grey's zombie novel was the straw that broke the camel's back. *Other writers offering far inferior work could get published, why couldn't he*, thought Grey.

Those bastards, those smug, self-satisfied bastards. They'd taken their books to the fabled 'Palace of Publishing,' snared an agent, secured a publisher, been paid an advance, and stepped into the express elevator to literary success. They thought they were so clever, with their story editors to sharpen their plots and their copy editors to tidy their punctuation. And here he was, still unrecognised, hawking his first three chapters to literary agents, who either brushed him aside or took his lovingly prepared proposal, and dumped it into the waste bin as soon as they got back to the office.

Things were going to change though, he'd show them, he'd show the lot of them. He had their addresses. They'd been published in error in the brochure of the Annual Suffolk Literary Festival. He'd got hold of petrol, rags and a number of old, wide mouthed milk bottles which he'd found in their galvanised crate on a farm rubbish heap.

He knew who would be first; that bastard, Mike Wattam. He didn't need the address list to find him; he'd known him for years, and his house was in a village only a few miles away. Four books he'd published, all detective novels, all earning the handsome royalties he boasted about every time they bumped into each other in the local supermarket. Bloody detective novels, not even proper literature. He might as well have been writing bodice rippers or chick lit under an assumed name. Why should he have all the gravy?

It was midnight, and Grey had driven to Wattam's village and parked as close to his house as he dared. He opened the boot of the car, half-filled four of the bottles with petrol, stuffed in the rags, and placed his Molotov cocktails into a supermarket shopping bag. He was all ready to 'toast' the Great Man.

The thin hedge scratched at him as he pushed through it and into the author's sizeable garden. The house loomed, a darker patch against the midnight sky. Wattam had only afforded it because he'd married the right partner, a spinster from the local farming community, a dumpy woman who hung on his every stupid word and probably thought he was a bloody genius. Good luck!

Grey approached the back of the house, stopped on the lawn and placed the bag of incendiaries at his feet. He took out a bottle and shook it to wet the rag. He struck a match, lit the rag and drew back his arm to throw the bottle through an upstairs window. Then he remembered the thatched roof. How could he have forgotten that the house was thatched; what a blaze it would make. The fire service would never arrive in time to put it out. It would even be visible from his own house three miles away, once he'd quit the scene.

The flaming missile somersaulted lazily upwards onto the roof. The thatch should have caught light instantly but it was still soaked from the previous night's heavy rain. The flaming bottle rolled back down the steep incline, bumped over the gutter and dropped two stories before smashing over Grey's head.

Instantly he was a man of flames, running in circles shouting, 'Mike, Mike, help me, help me,' before he crashed screaming back through the hedge and onto the lane. He struggled blindly towards the bridge, hoping to douse himself in the village stream, but after a dozen steps he fell to his hands and knees, crawled briefly forward, then collapsed and lay still. The flames slowly died and smoke drifted from his blackened flesh and charred clothing.

Back at the house a light came on at an upstairs window, it creaked open as Wattam thrust out his's tousled head, supported on his scrawny neck. He peered myopically into the darkness as he struggled with his spectacles, and sniffed the air.

'Rather late for a barbeque and all this noise,' he called out grumpily at whoever had disturbed his sleep. He paused to listen, when there was no answer he grunted, withdrew his head, closed the window and pulled the curtain.

***

The Moon shone over the timeless Suffolk village, with its stream, its humpbacked brick bridge and its round-towered flint church. Nothing moved in the author's garden or the churchyard it adjoined. There was peace, silence, and a surprisingly appetising smell of roasted meat.

THE WHEEL FIDDLE

Published by Short-Story.Me ezine on 29th July 2018

The melody drifted across the garden as she was picking fruit to make a summer pudding. She put down her basket, wiped the sweat from her forehead and walked around to the front of the cottage. The man stood waiting at her garden gate, he raised his cap. He had a strange stringed instrument tucked under his arm, there was a small metal handle sticking out of its base.

'Can I help you?' she asked.

'I've a raging thirst, ma'am, been walking half the day, I'd be grateful for a cup a water.'

He was a down-at-heel looking character, his clothes were worn and dusty, he was probably a labourer seeking work, still strong, but lean and weather-beaten.

She turned and walked back up the path to the cottage and gestured him to follow.

'Sit there on the garden bench while I get you a cup,' she said.

In the kitchen she poured the water and cut a piece of the cake she'd baked for her husband, the day before. When she came out, he took the cup and plate from her with a sigh.

'My name's Tom,' he said as he bit into the cake. 'Tom Buckland.'

'What's that contraption at the side of you?'

'It's a wheel fiddle, ma'am, some call it a hurdy gurdy. I earn an extra shillin' here and there with it.'

'Well, you can sing for your supper, then.'

He smiled to himself, 'I can do that for certain,' he said.

He finished his cake and picked up the wheel fiddle.

'Can I see it?' Alice asked. She held the old instrument with its strings and levers, it was scratched and chipped, but its ivory inlays and brass fittings hinted at its once having been beautiful. She stroked the curve of its body and handed it back to him.

He settled it onto his lap, turned the crank and fingered the keys. A strange wailing melody sounded. He began to sing - in a higher voice than she was expecting - and in a language she didn't recognise. Goose pimples rose on her arms and legs, the fine hairs on her spine stood up, and the feeling flowed up her back and on to the top of her head.

The traveller's dark brown eyes watched her unblinkingly as the song continued. Her knees turned to water, she sat down on the close-cropped lawn and lay back. The swifts and martins dipped and dived, racing and turning across the sky, she closed her eyes.

Waking suddenly as she heard her husband push open the garden gate, she could tell from the light that time had passed. There was no sign of the traveller, the plate and cup were neatly stacked on the bench.

'I thought I heard music,' said her man.

Alice stood up and brushed the creases from her dress. 'Music?' she asked.

***

The baby was born the next March, during lambing season, an inconvenient time for a shepherd's wife to be birthing a child. Her mother used to say, 'There's no good time to be having a baby,' and she was right.

A sensible shepherd stays away from his wife in July, and so her husband had, but he never spoke of the birth date, after all July was a long time back and it was hard to be sure. As the baby grew, it had his brown eyes and dark complexion. Alice called him Martin for the birds nesting under the eaves of the cottage last summer.

Martin grew to be ten years old. He went to the church school and had the adventures that country boys have. One day, he was running an errand for his mother to the village shop, when he heard music coming from round a bend in the road. He stood listening, presently a man appeared, his clothes were shabby, he was holding a strange device and cranking a handle as he walked, this was the source of the music. He stopped when he reached the boy and looked at him closely.

'Would you like to try?' he asked after a few moments.

They sat on the bank, and the man showed Martin how to press the keys and wind the handle.

'What's it called?' he asked.

'It's a wheel fiddle, boy, and you've a fair talent for it, so keep it, I've no use for it no more.' The traveller stood and continued on his way. The boy barely noticed him leave, the eerie music seemed to play itself as he walked slowly back to his parents' cottage. His mother came to the front door, ashen-faced.

'Where did you get that thing?' she snapped.

'A travelling man gave it to me, he said I have a talent for it,' and he carried on playing.

She felt the magic of the music once again, but she was older now and the resonance was weaker, but still the hairs on the back of her neck stood up.

'We'll have to see what your father says about it,' she said sternly, but then softened after a moment when she realised that the boy's father had already had his say.

PENANCE

Published by Sirens Call ezine 1st September 2018

He'd hung back, he was the last penitent of the day.

'Bless me, father, for I have sinned.'

'When was your last confession, my son?'

'Many years ago, father, thirty at least, not since I was fourteen.'

'And what has brought you back to the bosom of the church now, my son?'

'I'm going to kill somebody, and I wondered if I could get absolution for my sin?'

'I can't give you absolution for a sin you haven't committed, my son.'

'No, I thought you'd say that, father. Still, worth a try.'

'Why are you going to murder this person, my son?'

'Because he's been having an affair with my wife while I was serving in Afghanistan.'

'And you know this for certain?'

'Oh, yes, there are security cameras on the house. He's been parking at the back, right in front of one. Three times a week for the last six months. You've got to admire his enthusiasm.' He chuckled.

'Do you know who owns this car, my son?'

'Oh yes, father, my brother's a traffic cop. He looked the number up for me, told me the owner's name and address.'

'Perhaps the visits were purely innocent, my son. Perhaps it was a matter of friendly support while you were away.'

'Not according to my wife, father. Once I showed her the car on the computer screen, she broke down and told me all about it. Her loneliness, the visits from this friend. How he helped her, how the relationship developed, how he would give up everything so they could run away together. All the usual clichés that men tell women when they want to get them into bed.'

'And when did she tell you all this, my son?'

'About half an hour ago. I expect you keep your phone switched off when you're doing confessions, father? Wouldn't want any interruptions, would you? Perhaps you'd like to say a few Hail Marys now.'

The metallic rasp, as the penitent pulled back the slide of his automatic pistol, echoed around the empty church. As did the shot that followed it.

PRESSING MATTERS

Published by Sirens Call ezine 1st September 2018

'Oui, monsieur, how can I help?' asked the short, middle-aged woman, drying her hands on her apron as she answered her front door.

'Yes, this is the farm of Henri Bertauld. Unfortunately, my husband is away at the moment, visiting a sick relative, you understand. Ah, the wine, certainly, monsieur, it's been very popular: the wonderful summer last year, plenty of sugar in the grapes, the bouquet is marvellous.'

'A tasting? Nothing could be simpler, follow me, monsieur.' She led him along the path to the winery next door, a converted barn attached to the old stone farmhouse.

The visitor seemed impressed by the array of modern stainless-steel pipework and equipment, which was dominated by the massive hydraulic wine press. It was at odds with the traditional appearance of the exterior of the building.

Madam eyed the visitor. His dress and accent hinted at Paris and his arrogant manner confirmed it. He looked as if he might be worth a few cases so she pulled the cork on a fresh bottle and poured two half glasses, it would be bad manners to let him drink alone.

'À votre santé, monsieur.' They raised their glasses and looked each other in the eye for a moment. The visitor, of course, had to make a big show of holding the glass to the light, swirling the wine around, sniffing it, sipping it. He inflated his cheeks and moved it around his mouth as if it were mouthwash. At least he didn't spit it into a bucket. She took a small sip from her own glass and watched his reaction.

His expression passed from concentration to surprise, then pleasure, followed by something bordering on ecstasy.

Easy money, she thought to herself.

'So, six cases, monsieur, certainment, let me help you carry them to your car.'

The transaction complete, she waved him off from the doorway of the winery, then moved back inside, out of the heat. She sighed, took another sip of wine, then fumbled in the pocket of her apron for her tobacco and papers, rolled a cigarette, and sat down to enjoy the break from her housework.

Looking towards the wine press she thought about that bastard husband of hers, Henri Bertauld. She remembered his nickname for her, 'the toad'. She remembered the years of insults and verbal abuse, his penny pinching and, latterly, when he was in his cups, the beatings she had suffered at his hand. But she came from a patient stock, with the desert in her heritage. She knew that if she waited her moment would come eventually, and it did, with the last batch of grapes that season.

***

There had been a blockage in the outlet from the press, a foreign object hidden in the grapes. Bertauld had raised the piston and reached over the open press, holding a steel rod, poking and prodding in an attempt to clear it. He had leaned too far, the drunken fool, and over balanced. He'd fallen into the grapes and lay struggling on the surface, vainly trying to get his feet under him. It had taken only a moment for her to see her opportunity, make her decision, and press the start button.

She could still hear his roar of anger, followed by his threats and finally his pathetic pleadings and promises, as the motor whirred and the steel piston slowly but inexorably moved downwards, and pressed him into the grapes. His spluttering didn't last long. She remembered thinking it was lucky that the wine they made was red. Anyway, it was all over in a minute or two.

It had taken two days for her to decide on her next move. She'd sell the farm and disappear, go back to her family in Algeria. He would be someone else's problem. She'd leave him where he was, the pulp would ferment and preserve the body. The new owner would not discover it until he got around to emptying the press, maybe next spring, maybe later than that.

***

She stood up and walked back to the house, dropping her cigarette end on the path and pausing to crush it underfoot. She looked across the fields of vines. It had been another good summer. *This year's wine should be even better than last's*, she thought, chuckling to herself. *It would have more body this year.*

CURING BRIAN

Published by Short-Story.Me ezine 9th September 2018

The day started pleasantly enough: we'd met for our weekly game of tennis, the old dependables, Chris, Marilyn, Malcolm and me. Then the man in the dirty suit appeared, and everything changed.

It was summer and the weather was warm, so we'd used the outside court, the one next to the soccer pitch. We'd been playing for about fifteen minutes when I noticed a guy staggering towards us over the field. When he finally arrived, he stood at the chain link fence, staring through at us and smiling vacantly. His skin was pale as if he'd been saved from drowning, but his lips were cherry red. Saliva slowly dribbled down his chin and dripped onto the ground. He gripped the wire with both hands and stood there, making mewling sounds, his clothes torn and soiled, as if he'd been sleeping rough. At first we ignored him, but having him there was unnerving, I couldn't concentrate on my serve. I thought he was drunk or had learning difficulties and hoped someone would come and take him away. Chris saw himself as the 'silverback' and he went over to talk to him. When he didn't seem to make much progress, the rest of us joined him. Chris asked the guy if he needed help, but he just kept whining and gurgling, I called 911 on my cell but it went to voicemail after a dozen rings.

As we stood there, another visitor shuffled into sight from the direction of town. He had the same pale complexion and red lips, but there was blood on his chin and down the front of his shirt. He looked like the man who ran the hardware store. I took a closer look and realised that he *was* the guy from the hardware store.

We realised something strange was happening. I told the others I was going to the police headquarters, about five hundred yards away. I walked to my car, and Chris padlocked the gate after me. There was a disturbance from the other side of the court, half a dozen more weirdoes had arrived. They all wore police uniforms, but they were dishevelled, with torn shirts, no hats, ties askew, faces bloody. I nearly crapped myself, as I jumped in the car and locked the doors. Then the kids from the elementary school arrived, hundreds of them, tousled, bloody, moving slowly. They surrounded the court and hung on the wire mesh, whimpering and moaning, and looking sort of hungry.

I drove to the police station and looked around carefully before I got out of the car. The double doors were open, broken furniture and debris littered the foyer. Somewhere in the depths of the building an alarm was ringing. I climbed over the front desk and walked through the empty offices until I found the staircase. I worked my way up through the rooms on the next two stories to the top floor, searching for somebody, anybody. The door from the stairs to the top level was locked. I hammered hard and eventually a face appeared, a frightened face, then another three. They made me turn around to get a good look at me before they opened the door.

‘Do you know what’s happening?’ asked the blonde girl who I found out later was called Sally.

‘Not really, but look at that.’ We could see down into the tennis court from the office window. Marilyn, Chris and Malcolm were standing back to back in the centre of the court, holding their rackets in front of themselves like clubs. The weight of the zombies had flattened the fence, and they were slowly streaming over it. The whole town seemed to be out there. I watched in horrified fascination as the zombies slowly surrounded and overwhelmed my friends. A few minutes later the mob dispersed and there was no sign of them, they’d been absorbed.

***

All this was eight days ago. There are five of us up here, me and the four clerical workers, Wally, Sally, Brian and Sheila. We’ve secured the entrances at ground level and gathered all the food and water we can find. We spend a lot of the time on the flat roof of the building, vainly waiting for a helicopter to come and rescue us. Water won’t be a problem when the water cooler bottles run out: there are fire tanks up here. It’s the food I’m worried about. We haven’t got much of it, and small quantities keep disappearing. I’m sure it’s that fat bastard, Brian, who’s stealing it.

***

The hot weather reminds me of my time in South Africa, watching the bushmen cutting strips of meat from their kill, then drying it in the sun. They call it 'biltong,' it keeps for months. I look at Brian and think about quietly sliding a biscuit into his pocket and then denouncing him. I have one of the policemen's pistols, all I need is an excuse to use it.

PILGRIMAGE

Gained an Honourable Mention in the Writers of the Future competition October 2018

Published by AntipodeanSF ezine 1st October 2018

Broadcast on the AntipodeanSF Radio Show in 2019

Siblings, hatchlings, juveniles, we, your brood mates, send filial greetings and news of the successful completion of our sacred journey. These returners who carry our message back to you will guide you on the Pilgrimage next season.

Well can we remember our parting from the warmth and light of our home colony. How your good wishes and scintillating coruscations encouraged us as we set off across the cold and barren lands. Led by the steady lights of our guides we left the comforts of home and began our long and hungry passage through the darkness. We flashed and glimmered to each other to help keep our spirits up.

There were those that lost faith part way and turned back, but we had travelled far, and they had no one to guide them. I weep at the thought of these poor souls floundering helplessly through the blackness, their lights and signals flashing feebly and to no avail, finally to be extinguished as they succumbed to the dark and loneliness. I pray that they stayed together and could give each other some consolation at their ending.

The rest of us kept the faith and pushed on. After long journeying and many trials, we arrived, hungry, cold and exhausted. We fell into the welcoming arms of the Guardians of the Perimeter of the fabled City. Strong and armed though they were, they took us to the House of Healing. There they comforted us, stroked us, gave us food, watched over us as we rested and regained our strength. Once we had all recovered, we were ready to observe the rituals and complete our Pilgrimage.

Guides came and led us to a cliff overlooking the City of the Queen. How can I describe its beauty? The fragile splendour of the towers shedding light and warmth from above. The beautiful curves of the streets and plazas, the parklands and buildings and, at its centre, the ring wall of the Queen's Palace.

Our guides took us to see the first ritual, the Parade of Strength, in the central plaza. We watched as our soldiers displayed themselves in red and black, silver highlights shining as they moved in geometric patterns, their actions jerky and synchronized. Each squad performing their own fighting routine, some with weapons, others without. How we gasped and quivered, our colours reflecting those of the warriors as we were drawn into their display. Several of our party were so affected by the sight that their colours became fixed and, after much twining and caressing, they left us to join the soldiers. We respect their choice in giving up the Pilgrimage.

The guides led us on to the Palace of Tears. Words fail me as I try to tell you of the pathetic sights we saw within its smooth and graceful interior: the twisted limbs and bodies, the monsters with several heads, the giants, the dwarfs, the imbeciles. How we wept in the presence of these poor benighted, malformed creatures, our brothers, members of the Chosen. We showed our sympathy, adopting the restful blues and greens of the carers. With their colours flowing gently up and down their limbs, some of our number elected to stay and help these unfortunates. We writhed and flashed goodbyes to our brood mates and wished them well.

It was a great relief to enter the Theatre of Laughter. There were creatures of all types, including the Chosen. They performed tricks and stunts, and made garish, seemingly impossible - and sometimes highly inappropriate - combinations of colours. Several members of the group were shocked but others mirrored their displays and, with reassuring movements, they left to join the Theatre's company while we continued the Pilgrimage.

Our guides led us to the Arena of Light, where all the remaining pilgrims, from all the colonies, gathered to share the Miracle of Choosing. We drifted high towards the dazzling illumination of the upper reaches, and some were taken but most were not. We hid our disappointment with shows of fluorescence and blushes of many hues. Then, after dallying as long as our guides allowed us, we moved on to the next ritual, flashing and blinking our gossip as we followed them.

They led us to the Museum of Mysteries where there were displays of strange, metallic artefacts, their forms were regular and unnatural: straight edges, cylinders, spheres. Some reflective, others not, some generated heat or light from within, others were cold and lifeless. They had been found and transported across the dark and barren lands to the City. We could only guess at their provenance and functions,

What a relief it was to enter the Library of Smiles. Here we could examine the shapes and colours left behind by earlier pilgrims. Our guides encouraged us to leave messages of goodwill and happiness. They gave us food, and we rested before the culmination of our Pilgrimage: The Dance of Love and Light. Suddenly our guides became agitated, they had received word. *She* was ready. With flashes of excitement and arousal, they herded us to the Palace of the Queen.

We approached the walls of obsidian and began the circular dance. Hundreds of pilgrims, thousands, joined in from all directions, flashing and sparkling dazzling displays of colour combinations never expressed until now. We soared and looped in our rapture, becoming creatures of light and flight and weightlessness. We drifted above the perimeter wall through milky clouds as the Queen released her eggs and we gave ourselves to her. Millions and millions of glistening opalescent pearls rose, combining and clumping into groups, drifting away to form colonies of their own, if conditions favoured them. How we flashed and scintillated our encouragement to them, knowing most would be lost in the dark lands. Only those that found an empty colony with its towers of light and warmth would prosper.

Soon, the Dance was over and we drifted, our displays dim and subdued, a numbness, a lassitude suffused us all. Our guides led us to the Well of Endings where, waiting on its rim, before we began our spiral descent, we chose the strongest pilgrims to return to the home colony with this, our message of hope.

'Siblings, we have completed the Pilgrimage, served our purpose, stayed strong and delivered our precious contribution to the Queen. Pray that you too will have success in your turn when you follow us. Now we will descend into the dark and warmth, hoping only for rest and tranquillity, peace and forgetfulness. Our journey is over, yours yet to begin. May Fate and Circumstance smile upon you.

Remember that more is expected of you than of most, for you are the Chosen. We salute you.'

STAR SIGN

Published by 365Tomorrows ezine 25th March 2018

Published by AntipodeanSF ezine 1st July 2018

Broadcast on AntipodeanSF Radio Show 3rd Nov 2018

'So, what's your star sign?' Mary asked, and took a sip from her glass, she watched him closely over the rim. It was one of her stock questions on first dates. You could tell a lot about a man, depending on how he reacted. His actual star sign was irrelevant, she didn't believe in astrology.

She liked to meet new prospects in the pub, on the way home from work. It was easy to make a hasty exit after one polite drink if the 'Perfect Match' was less than perfect. And, let's face it, most of them were, it was just a matter of degree.

'I'm not sure, I think you call it Antares.'

'There isn't a star sign called Antares,' she said. She picked up her glass and appraised him as she took another sip.

He touched his ear and paused for a few seconds as if listening. 'Oh, what star *sign,'* he said, 'a subgroup of a horoscope of twelve.'

'Yes, which one are you?' she asked again, trying not to show her irritation.

'I'm a Monkey,' he said. He tried his drink, tentatively, as if he'd never tasted beer before and was finding it difficult to acquire a taste for it.

'A Monkey?'

He paused and touched his ear again, 'Oh, sorry, wrong horoscope, I'm an Aquarian, born on the twenty-fourth of January.' He looked around the pub and smiled as he scrutinised the décor of old agricultural implements, tools and horse brasses hanging from the beams and walls.

'Such an old technology,' he said. 'Hard to believe that you still use human and quadruped muscle to power your food production.'

'We don't, they're antiques,' she said. She thought he was rather gauche but he was pleasant enough looking, about her age (thirty), nicely slim and well presented. She even liked the smell of his aftershave, which she hadn't yet identified, and she was something of an expert on men's aftershaves. She came to a decision: he'd do, certainly for a night, after that, time would tell.

She put her drink back down on the table. 'Would you like to come back to my place?' she asked. 'It's quieter there and we could get to know each other better,'

'Oh, yes, I've been looking forward to this,' he said, 'I've never been on a two-sex planet before.'

Oh no, she thought, a first timer, I'll have to explain everything to him step by step – it'll ruin the spontaneity.

'Never mind,' she said, downing her gin and tonic. 'I think I'll pass on this one.' She stood, picked up her handbag and left.

I'm going to stick to Tinder Vanilla in future, she thought, as she walked to the car park. *Tinder Galactica is just too unpredictable*.

'Car open,' she said and climbed in as the door sighed up. 'Car home,' she said, it set off, almost soundlessly. There was no point being polite to software, particularly if it wasn't even sentient.

Oh well, she thought, *another night in with the rabbit, and maybe some screen time later. You can't win 'em all.*

CRASH DUMMY

Published by Altered Reality Magazine 5th Dec 2018

It wouldn't be a long flight, and I hoped that the aisle seat next to me would stay empty, but no such luck, a young woman took it. I checked her over as she lifted her bag up to the overhead locker. You can't help it: I mean, I may be a priest but I still have a full set of human instincts, although these days, thank God, age has blunted some of them, made them easier to handle. She nodded to me as she took her seat, she was very attractive, wearing a black business suit with a short jacket and knee-length skirt. I decided to include her in my prayers, always my policy when I see a good-looking woman: I pray that their beauty doesn't lead them into sin. I'd talked about this years ago at the seminary near Dublin with my confessor, Father George. Truth be told it had been his idea, and it seemed to work for me.

After take-off I dozed for a while. When I awoke, I half-opened my eyes and saw that my companion was mouthing silently and moving her fingers. Was she praying, saying the Rosary? Perhaps she was a nervous flier. As I moved, she looked over and smiled. 'I hope I didn't wake you, Father, I was just finishing my report.'

Report? It was the first time I'd heard praying referred to as that, and I was in the business, so to speak, perhaps it was some new slang I'd not heard. I couldn't place her accent. Perhaps English wasn't her mother tongue, and she'd learned the language with a British accent, rather than the more usual American.

The flight attendant brought drinks, he told us we'd be landing at Santiago in about an hour. 'We'll be down before that,' said my companion. She stared into her gin and tonic for a moment, then looked up and offered me her hand.

'My name's Farina, at least that's my original's name.'

Original name, did she mean her maiden name. She smiled brightly and asked me why I was flying to Santiago. I told her I was visiting my sister who lived in Valparaiso. We chatted about this and that and I told her the story of my sister's whirlwind romance with her Chilean boyfriend, after they'd met on a blind date. It was twenty years ago, when they were both working in London, but women love to hear about that sort of thing. I asked her what she did for a living.

'I'm an air crash investigator,' she said.

I was impressed. 'So, you must have had a lot of training for that.'

'My original did.'

Original, again, I was puzzled, but years of listening to confessions had taught me to let people talk, and things would usually become clear in the end.

'So, do you investigate all sorts of air crashes or do you specialise?' I was just making conversation, she had amber-coloured eyes, unusual and quite captivating.

'Well, Farina does. She specialises in unexplained commercial aviation accidents of the early 21st century.'

'I haven't heard of any air crashes in South America recently.'

'No, but there'll be one soon,' she said.

'Really, so you know which planes are going to crash beforehand?' I chuckled as I raised my glass to my lips.

'On this occasion, yes, because it'll be this one.' The plane bumped at just that moment, it took me by surprise, but it was nothing. I mopped at my spilt drink with a tissue. 'I've found that some of the navigation systems are wrongly calibrated, and there is an unusual wind shear in the Jetstream.' She stared at me intently. 'The pilots think they're travelling faster than they are. Then there's the fog over the mountains that we need to cross. It all adds up, it's always a combination of factors that lead to an accident.' She nodded sagely and appeared to relax. 'The pilots will try to land too early and fly into a mountain. The plane will disappear, so I conjecture it will be covered by ice and snow. Difficult terrain, impossible to find, unusually the flight recorder will be destroyed.' She sat back and looked at me, 'What a shame there isn't room for us to fool around. I'd like to have tried it once.' There was a wistfulness in her voice.

I hoped she was joking, she could see my dog collar, although it isn't always as big a deterrent as you might think. Just for a moment an inappropriate picture of the two of us came into my mind. I really would have to include her in my prayers as soon as possible.

I took a slow sip of my single malt. 'How could you possibly know all this before it's actually happened?' I was beginning to feel uncomfortable sitting next to her. We hadn't been given an inflight meal, so, thankfully, there was no plastic cutlery around – I knew a man who was killed with a sharpened tooth brush when I worked as a prison chaplain.

'Well, Father,' she leaned closer. 'Actually, I'm a synthetic, an artificial person.'

'A synthetic? You mean you were grown in a tank? Like in the movies?' I laughed quietly, but she didn't. I looked around to see if there were any flight attendants nearby in case I needed any help. Unfortunately, they were all busy towards the back of the plane: there seemed to be some sort of medical emergency, an overweight male passenger lay in the aisle with people gathered around him. I could go down there and offer to give him extreme unction, I might be safer.

'Yes, Father, grown for this assignment.'

I wondered if she was making this up as she went along, or was she suffering a long-term delusion. She didn't *seem* delusional.

I pointed at her glass and tried to crack her logic, 'Do synthetics need to drink?'

'It's just a social convention, I can void food and liquids later.'

She was so attractive, perhaps she was an entertainer of some sort, maybe this was a spoof laid on by my "friends" at the seminary. I looked around but couldn't see anyone using their smartphone to film us. I tried a different tack.

'So, how come you can tell me all this? Isn't it against the rules, against the Prime Directive, so to speak?'

'You'd be right under normal circumstances, Father, but as we have such a short time left, and there will be no survivors....' She left the rest unsaid.

'No survivors? How do you *feel* about that?' I was remembering one of the many counselling courses I'd taken over the years.

'I've transmitted all the data and fulfilled my function. Copies get deleted, it's just a fact of life. My original lives on, that should be all that matters.' I noticed there were tears in her eyes. 'But the thing is, Father, it seems such a waste. I could have had a life. I'm not supposed to feel like this, there must have been a mistake in the copying process. Synths of my grade are not supposed to have emotions.' She began weeping quietly.'

I put an arm around her. 'There, there, my child, don't upset yourself. Now tell me, is there any medication that you're supposed to be taking? Let's just have a little look in your purse, here.' The lighting dimmed as we started losing height and slid into the cloud bank covering the Andes.

'Ladies and Gentlemen, the Captain has illuminated the seat belt signs as we are beginning our descent into Santiago International airport. Please ensure that your seat back and folding tray are in the upright position,' said the recorded voice.

I couldn't find any medication, so I comforted the "crash dummy" and wondered idly if a "synthetic person" could have a soul. It would make for an interesting discussion with my students next semester.

Our seats were near the front of the plane, the security door to the flight deck opened, and a young pilot, most probably the first officer, stepped out and looked anxiously down the aisle towards the knot of people gathered around the fallen passenger.

Suddenly, behind him, an alarm began to warble and I heard a robotic voice repeating: '*Pull up, pull up, pull up, pull up....*'

PART THREE

The Fly on the Wall

THE FLY ON THE WALL

Published by CommuterLit ezine – 18th September 2018

This story is a chapter taken from my time travel novel 'Chronoscape.'

UK the 2040s

Mary Lee walked across the parade ground at RAF Waddington. Although she moved purposefully and wore her smart Air Force blues, she had a hangover from her weekend activities in the officers' mess. Being young and single, indulging in the three D's - Drinking, Dancing and Dating - was pretty much mandatory. She noted the activities around her. Vehicles carried personnel and supplies from one part of the station to another. There was a shrieking from the engine test bays and the smell of jet fuel. Looking up, she watched a pair of fighters execute an impossibly sharp and noisy turn. There could be no humans on board, they'd be unconscious from the g-force. Artificial intelligences have taken over all the best jobs. She sighed and tried to put the thought out of her head as she entered the operations building to start her shift. In the changing rooms her ear lobe tingled, her software sprite spoke quietly in her ear.

'The boss wants you in his office, ma'am.' Its familiarity level was set to 'respectful'; there was no point in being friendly with software that wasn't even self-aware.

'Okay, tell him I'm on my way,' she sub-vocalized. After buttoning her jacket, she ran a hand through her bobbed black hair and walked back to the admin area. The Group Captain's door was ajar, he was standing talking to a civilian, so she knocked and waited in the doorway. Her boss beckoned her in.

'This is Flying Officer Lee, Dr Abrahams,' he said. 'Dr Abrahams is over from Langley, Mary.' She shook hands with the newcomer. He was the same height as her, short for a man, about sixty, and lightly built. Mary thought he looked like a jockey. 'Dr Abrahams is a scientist with a 'special interest.' I'd like you to show him the drone control room, answer any of his questions and bring him back in an hour, we have to attend a meeting later.'

Mary knew better than to ask about Abraham's 'special interest,' he was obviously a spook if he worked at Langley. His English accent suggested he wasn't CIA, perhaps he was SIS, the UK's Secret Intelligence Service.

'I understand you're a drone pilot,' said Abrahams, making conversation as they walked along the corridor. They entered the control room with its dozen black upholstered couches and racks of related equipment. 'What type of drones do you fly?'

'Small ones,' she said, and took him over to a mahogany display case. It contained an array of dead, but carefully mounted flies, of various types and sizes, from the humble house fly, to a large horse fly. They were labelled with both their Latin and their common names. 'If you look closely, you can see that their thoraxes are enlarged.' Abrahams looked blankly at the display, Mary pointed to the squadron emblem on the wall. It depicted a member of the same genus 'diptera,' with the motto 'Non muscae super me.' 'No flies on me,' she joked.

'Oh, those are the drones. Well, I'm impressed by the miniaturization.' He peered at the specimens with more interest. 'Are they real insects or fabrications?' he asked.

'They're modified insects. No point in re-inventing the wheel when the natural version is so efficient.' Thinking she might have sounded sarcastic, she continued in a more careful tone. 'They insert a small pack of quantum electronics at the pupal stage, while the maggot's anatomy has melted into an organic soup. As the adult insect forms, the pack makes millions of connections into its central nervous system, and 'bish bash bosh,' you have your drone. It's more complicated than that, but I only have to know enough to fly the little buggers. They don't need any maintenance, they die after a few weeks, and we get issued with replacements as necessary. The wranglers look after them, feed them, transport them around. They have insectaries all over the country. The electronics are easy to produce so the drones are cheap to manufacture.' Mary picked up a virtual reality visor and put it on. She turned its mirrored surface towards him, hoping to surprise him with the distorted reflection of his own face.

'What does it feel like when you're flying them?'

She sat on the couch. 'As pilots, we have total sensory integration and control. When I lie back like this, put on my visor and place my hands in these sensor depressions, I am the fly.' The visor muffled her voice.

'But how can you handle six legs and two wings?'

'The software handles many of the functions, we point our host in the direction we want to go and the computer does the rest. It's not that different from riding a horse. Probably more like being a centaur because you're integrated with your host's nervous system.'

Abrahams was about to ask something else when the next shift arrived, wearing their black sensuits. The pilots began to get into position on the couches, their orderlies checking their straps and connections before fitting visors over their faces.

'While we inhabit our hosts, we're not exactly high dependency patients, but we need to be monitored. That's why we have orderlies. The restraints are necessary too, you wouldn't want to act out the movements of your host while you're piloting. It can happen if the feedback filters are tuned out of resonance, like sleep walking.' She vacated the couch as its scheduled occupant arrived, smiling, followed by her orderly, a corporal burdened with her visor and other equipment. They left the control room and walked down the corridor to the canteen. Abrahams ordered coffee as they sat at a table. Mary drank hers gratefully, her headache diminished, either from the caffeine or the hydration, she didn't care which.

'How secret is the fly drone program? I wasn't aware of it, I expected something bigger and more mechanical.'

'Very secret,' she said. 'We get all sorts of requests from SIS and MI5. Sometimes we leave flies in odd corners and on lampshades, curled up and apparently dead, but their electronics can still function as surveillance devices for weeks. I heard of a pilot who flew a drone into an enemy's code room and landed on an operator's shoulder. He recorded the clear data as the operator typed it into the encryption program. The enemy assumed we'd broken their code and had to change all their security protocols, very disruptive and expensive for them.'

'What about assassination,' he asked hesitantly, 'are they ever used for that?'

Ah, thought Mary, *one of them*. A pity, he'd seemed alright until now.

'There have been stories of horse flies being adapted to deliver poisons: they have a strong bite so you could prime their jaws. I suppose you could use wasps with a modified poison in their sting. There could be another team doing that sort of thing but I'm not aware of it. I'm currently on 'Royalty Protection' keeping an eye on Prince George and his family.'

'How did you get involved in the first place?' asked Abrahams.

'I trained as a fighter pilot, but as they use AIs to fly most military aircraft now, it isn't easy to get a seat flying anything. They offered me this; it was a big change from flying jets to flying insects though.'

'Now, every time I see a spider or a fly, I'll wonder if it's spying on me and reporting back,' laughed Abrahams. 'I'll be adding fly spray to my office supplies list. In future I want it to be a no-fly zone. Are you all right, you've gone quite pale?'

'Not spiders,' she said with a shudder. 'Arachnids don't go through a pupal stage, so we can't insert the little box of tricks into them. No, not spiders, you're safe from being spied on by them.'

He laughed, ' "Spiders, spied on," very good.'

Holding her emotions in close control she took him back to the Group Captain's office for his meeting.

Mary went to the changing room, she needed a few moments alone. Sitting on a bench with her head in her hands, she remembered the horrifying incident two years before, when the spider had caught her. She was on 'Royalty Protection' at Clarence House, spying on Diana the Queen Mother. The Establishment hated her and watched her every move. Mary had been following her from a reception room to her bedroom, flying just below the high ceiling, when she found herself entangled in the sticky cables of a web. Puzzled at first, as she bounced back and forth, it was a few moments before she activated the disengagement procedure. The software was slow, and she lived through the horror of the first few seconds, helpless, as the enormous, hairy, grey beast approached, its strange array of shiny black eyes unblinking, its palps quivering. It grabbed her and stuck its foot-long fangs into her poor body, turning her insides to liquid pain as its venom and digestive juices did their work. Then she was spinning round and round as her attacker wrapped her in a gossamer shroud. Helpless and disorientated, she screamed silently.

The system bumped her out, but her heart rate and other vital signs had gone into the red. It had only taken a few seconds, but it had seemed much longer. Groggily she returned to consciousness, an alarm was sounding nearby. She could move her head but the wrist and ankle straps still held her.

'Doctor, doctor, over here quickly, she's having a fit,' her orderly was shouting. *Maureen's panicking,* she thought, *that's not a good sign.*

Dr Tom came and sat on the orderly's seat. 'Don't worry Mary, you're back now,' his voice was calm, and she heard the hiss of the aerosol on her arm. 'You'll feel much better in a few seconds.' He held her hand while the drug took effect, and she felt herself floating away, Maureen removed her visor and undid her restraints.

Several hours later, she woke up in the psychological evaluation unit. She lay entranced by the shadows cast by the gentle light shining through the venetian blinds as they moved slowly across the wall opposite her bed. An hour passed before the medics noticed that she was fully conscious. They brought her a cup of tea, how glorious it tasted. She sighed contentedly and leaned forward as a nurse plumped her pillows.

They kept her sedated for two days before they started the therapy. She never got the pictures out of her head but the treatment helped her to live with them, most of the time.

A week later, Mary was sitting in the hospital day room when the unit's civilian software engineer came to see her. Patrick worked for General Electronics, the drone control system's manufacturer. He was a quiet, dark haired, good-looking, young man. She had spoken to him before from time to time and he often led the update training on the squadron. He asked after her health, looked suitably sympathetic and then explained his visit.

'They want me to find a way of avoiding all this trauma,' he said. 'We can't exterminate spiders, but we can make the system bump the pilots out quicker, before they experience the spider attack. Currently the decoupling routines are too slow, and disengaging abruptly is also unpleasant and dangerous, like ejecting out of a cockpit. I want to make it fast and safe.'

'What will you use as the trigger?' she asked.

'It'll be the moment that the fangs touch the fly's epidermis, and then it's probably just a matter of putting in a software buffer. That's what I'll try first.'

An hour later, when he had all the information he needed, he said goodbye, and left. The next afternoon he returned.

'How are you today?' he asked as he sat opposite her in the dayroom. Mary put down her magazine.

'I thought you'd finished interviewing me,' she said, pretending not to see the flowers that lay across his lap (he might have just called in to clarify something on the way to visit his mother.)

'Well, I'm not here on official business,' he said as he handed them to her.

'How nice,' she held them to her face and inhaled. 'I love the smell of freesias. It reminds me of my childhood. My grandmother used to grow them on her balcony, back in Singapore. Mum and I used to visit her every year, and there was always the scent of freesias hanging in the air.' Mary realized that warm tears were running down her cheeks. She put a hand to her forehead and wept quietly for a moment, Patrick passed the box of tissues from the side table.

'I'm sorry, they've taken me off the tranks and my emotions haven't settled yet, they warned me this might happen.'

Patrick moved over to her sofa, took the flowers and put his arm around her shoulders.

'This isn't very military of me,' she said.

'It's alright, you've been through a terrible experience, like something out of a horror movie. Hardly anybody else has experienced anything as alien and awful as being attacked by a giant spider. The only other person I can think of is Frodo Baggins.'

'He doesn't count, he's a fictional character,' she said. They both laughed.

Patrick visited her every day, and when she returned to work a few weeks later they started to see each other socially. After a couple of months Mary moved in with him - sharing a bed helped a lot in the small hours, when the nightmares came.

Tied up, lying helpless in total darkness, unable to move, she sensed a nameless silent horror slowly approaching. She screamed and struggled with her bonds, but they were too strong. There were delicate, feathery probings at her throat and collar bone. The next thing would be the fangs, rapiers pushing relentlessly through the base of her neck and down behind her ribcage, into her heart and lungs, before the filthy, burning poisons were injected. Mary thrashed wildly and tried to scream.

Suddenly she was aware of the sheet wrapped tightly around her, the mattress supporting her, and the warmth of Patrick's body next to her. After disentangling herself, she rolled onto her back and lay panting, waiting for her pulse to stop hammering. She wiped her forehead, her sprite told her that it was four in the morning, Patrick was still asleep, she moved across the bed and spooned into his back. He smelled of sweat and aftershave. She felt such comfort with him beside her. He was a gentle soul on the surface, but strong and dependable underneath. As she calmed down, her thoughts returned to a conversation she'd had with her shrink, a few weeks earlier.

***

'I've never been phobic about spiders,' she'd said. 'In the tropics, I've seen really big ones, as big as your hand. I was brought up to respect spiders of all sizes, because even the small ones might be poisonous, but I'm not afraid of them on a day-to-day basis.' Mary walked over to a corner of the room where a long-legged house spider hung in a web near the ceiling. She made a cage of her hands, caught it gently, carried it over and dropped it onto his desk. He flinched and moved his chair back as the spider ran to the edge and abseiled to the floor. *Physician, heal thyself*, she thought as she sat down again.

'It's when I'm working, always expecting one to creep up on me, the thought of having to go through all that horror again, I hate it, I can't concentrate on the job, I'm always looking over my shoulder, or would be, if a fly had a shoulder.'

‘But you’ve told me that your drone has been caught by a bird. You said it’s a fairly common occurrence in the summer.’ He was peering around at the floor and had pulled his feet under his chair.

‘Yes, but if you’re caught by a swallow or a swift, your host dies instantaneously. You find yourself “back in the room,” lying on your couch, almost at once. It’s physically unpleasant for a few seconds, but spiders are a different matter, they make you suffer.’ A soft chime sounded.

‘Right, well, we can continue this on Tuesday,’ he said, nodding encouragingly as his keyboard appeared in front of him. Mary stood up and walked towards the door, she spotted the spider running madly across the floor, seeking the safety of the skirting board. She stepped on it, ground it into the carpet and glanced back: the shrink was watching, he looked down, began tapping at his keyboard, and moved his feet back in front of him.

***

She lay in the dark next to Patrick, worrying about the next day: they’d be testing the beta copy of his new software, she wasn’t looking forward to it.

Now she was in the shower, they were crawling out of the shower head and the drain, crawling all over her. She was screaming and stamping on them, but more and more came, no matter how many she killed, bigger and bigger, climbing up her legs, over her body, onto her face. She couldn’t kill them fast enough. They were in her hair, biting her scalp as she tried to tear them off. She closed her eyes and mouth but they forced their way in. Small ones were creeping into her ears, her nostrils.

She woke with a jerk and sat up gasping.

'I'll get you a glass of water,' said Patrick. He went into the bathroom as she lay panting, then came back, sat on her side of the bed and handed her the glass. 'It'll go away eventually,' he said. 'It'll just take time but you'll be alright in the end.' She drank, then put the glass on the bedside table, he got in next to her and put his arms around her. 'I'll look after you, Mary,' he whispered. 'It's my job. Go to sleep, it'll be better in the morning.' He pulled the covers over them both and she drifted off again.

The next day, Mary lay trembling slightly on her couch as her orderly checked everything for the third time. *Now I know how Anne Boleyn felt on her last morning*, she thought. *I do not want to do this, but I have to show Patrick that I have faith in him*.

'I'm sure everything's okay, Corporal, stop fussing around,' Mary snapped, then said more gently, 'Sorry, Maureen, I'm very grateful for your help.'

The orderly shrugged and smiled, 'That's alright ma'am, I'd be feelin' edgy meself.'

This is as bad as root canal work, Mary thought, and tried to control her shaking. If the software worked, it would give her confidence for the future, and she had every reason to believe it would work. It had worked when Patrick stuck a tiny pin into her captive drone yesterday. Mary had found herself 'back in the room' as soon as he touched her host's dermis.

Today's test was the real thing though. Her host was in one part of a plastic box in the next room, she felt sorry for it: the box was divided into two sections by a thin separator, in the other half sat a big, grey, garden spider. Patrick had caught it a week earlier and had shown her its impressive markings; he hadn't fed it since its capture.

'Okay, ma'am?' asked her orderly as she presented Mary's visor. Mary nodded and lifted her head.

She lay back and spoke to her sprite. 'Let's get this over with.'

'I'm sorry, ma'am, I don't under.....'

'Initiate insertion,' she interrupted.

A few moments later, Mary was standing on a smooth vertical surface, stable on her six sticky feet. She moved around until she could see the separator.

'Patrick wants to know if he can start?' said her sprite.

'Okay, go,' she said, and watched as, a moment later, the separator flipped up out of the way. The spider was enormous, it horrified her. She felt her host's agitation, but held it in check as its wings buzzed and it tried to flee. The spider jerked as it saw her, and then paused. It raised its front legs and slowly began to approach, its movements unbearably menacing. She saw lights reflected in its cluster of polished jet eyes, the spiky hairs that covered it, its jaws working. Mary couldn't face it and turned off her vision channel. She waited in the darkness as her unseen assailant crept up on her and struck.

And she was back in the room, jerking on her restraints and shouting, 'FUCK,' as she tried desperately to shake off her visor. Her orderly whisked it away and Dr Tom was already sitting on the jump seat holding her arm, ready with his aerosol. Patrick was hovering anxiously nearby.

'I'm okay,' said Mary breathlessly, 'I'm okay, I didn't feel a thing. It worked just fine, but I couldn't handle the sight of the spider as it closed in on me.' She was shallow panting. Dr Tom stood back and looked at her vital signs, on the screen above the couch, the aerosol wand held at his side. Maureen stepped in and undid the Velcro straps, with some difficulty because the stitching had been partly ripped.

'They'll need repairing,' she pointed them out to the Doctor. 'I've never seen anything like it, it can't be good for her.' She sponged sweat from Mary's face, and helped her up. Patrick supported her, as she walked slowly towards the changing rooms.

'It wasn't my idea,' said the Doctor, as Maureen busied herself wiping the couch and tidying up. He sighed and walked back to his office, shaking his head.

PART FOUR

Steampunk Confederation

1 - HARRY LAMPETER

First episode published by Literally Stories ezine 8th August 2018

First episode published by AntipodeanSF ezine 1st November 2018

First episode broadcast on the AntipodeanSF Radio Show in 2019

Harry Lampeter knelt by the side of his Norton motorcycle, laid his Lee-Enfield over the saddle, and sighted at the airship as it chuffed past, half a mile away. The musket was a new design with a rifled barrel. His shot hit the airship's boiler and a jet of steam and water gushed out. The rear propeller slowed and stopped almost at once. The ship was at the mercy of the wind. Its pilot, Telford Stephenson, would have to land and make repairs if he wanted to deliver the stolen Ironclad warship plans to the rebel government in the North. Harry Lampeter, being an agent of the British Government in

London, had no intention of letting Telford deliver the plans to Edinburgh, the Northern Alliance's capital city.

Telford evidently hadn't heard the shot over the sound of the steam engine. Lampeter watched as he started the Helium compressors and the airship lost height. He mounted his motorcycle and followed at a safe distance, riding on and off-road as necessary.

A few miles ahead, the airship passed over a farmer walking his ploughing team home. Telford shouted down to him, then threw out a rope. Lampeter watched as he spoke to the farmer, then lowered down a sack of what had to be salt or sugar, currency these days. The farmer hitched the rope to the team of horses and they hauled the airship towards the farmhouse, visible in the valley below them. Half an hour later Lampeter saw Telford securing the dirigible with ropes and pegs near the entrance to the barn, presumably he needed its workshop facilities.

Lampeter found a hill that overlooked the farm, lay down, pulled out his telescope, and kept watch on Telford for the next few hours, as he shaped a copper patch and cleaned the mating surfaces before he soldered it onto the boiler. As darkness fell Telford stopped, washed in a horse trough, then knocked on the farmhouse door. The farmer's wife answered, she was a plump, middle-aged woman, drying her hands on her apron as she gestured him inside.

Seeing his chance, Lampeter walked quietly down the hill, climbed into the airship's open gondola and searched for the stolen Ironclad warship's plans. He found them rolled up in a leather drawing tube strapped to the pedestal of the ship's wheel. He had taken them out and stuffed them into the side pocket of his leather riding coat when he felt the barrel of a revolver jabbed roughly into his back.

'I'll take them if you don't mind,' said Telford, chuckling. 'You don't think I could mistake a bullet hole for a blown seam, do you? Besides,' he held up the lead slug he'd found embedded in his boiler and raised an eyebrow. 'I'm glad it's you though Harry, I owe you a favour, since you carried me back over the lines to your field hospital, at the battle of Lincoln.'

'How did you escape?' asked Lampeter.

'I didn't, they patched me up and sent me home as part of a prisoner exchange.'

'Presumably, you were all sworn not to take part in hostilities again,' said Lampeter.

Telford shrugged, he stepped back, keeping the revolver aimed steadily at his prisoner's midriff.

'Turn around and put these on,' he said as he threw over a pair of handcuffs. 'You can sleep in the barn; the farmer will release you in the morning.' He gestured with the gun and Lampeter walked through the large open doors. Telford roped his handcuffs to a beam above his head, it wouldn't be a comfortable night.

In the morning he could hear Telford fussing with the airship's boiler and getting up steam. There was a conversation between him and the farmer, then the chuffing of the airship's engine slowly receded as it gained height. The farmer came in and unlocked the cuffs. Lampeter walked out of the barn rubbing life back into his wrists and looked up at the airship gaining height. At about a thousand feet, the aneroid triggers fired the charges he'd planted.

The two rear support ropes parted, and the gondola fell from a horizontal to a vertical configuration. He could see Telford clinging to the wheel for dear life, his legs dangling and kicking, his top hat falling.

The engine and boiler ripped free and fell towards the ground, there was a satisfyingly large steam explosion as they hit. The airship, freed from much of its ballast, began a rapid ascent towards the stratosphere. Lampeter could hear Telford's screams and wondered if he would use his parachute or regain control before he reached fifteen thousand feet, the asphyxiation limit. Telford wasn't a bad sort. As youngsters, they'd both been scholars at the Royal Hospital Naval Academy, near Ipswich. They'd played on the same Rugby team and there had been a certain amount of mutual experimentation in the showers. Anyway, Lampeter didn't want him dead. It was part of the London Government's plan that Harry retrieve the original drawings and substitute counterfeits for delivery to the Northern Alliance. The ones he had handed to Telford specified an increase in the thickness of the armour plating that would leave the Ironclad battleship top heavy. It would almost certainly capsize when they launched it from the slipway of whichever Govan shipyard it was built in. He looked forward to reading about it in the Telegraph in about two years' time. He imagined a Daguerreotype image of the ship lying across the Clyde, rendering the river unnavigable. That would give the Celtic allies something to think about.

Lampeter patted the pocket of his coat and felt the wad of original plans safely deposited where he'd hidden them just before Telford captured him.

Telford's top hat, complete with leather driving goggles, fell at his feet. He reached down, picked it up, examined it for damage and, finding none, placed it on his head, giving it a cheery pat.

'You'll be wantin' your breakfast then, supposin' ye can pay for it,' said the farmer.

'No thanks old chum, I'll have it at my club,' said Lampeter as he strode off, bell-bottom trousers flapping.

***

A few minutes later, the farmer heard a motorcycle start. He saw it set off on the London road, the stranger's long hair trailed out behind him, he was wearing the hat and goggles. The hat blew off, and the farmer made a note to retrieve it later.

2 - TELFORD STEPHENSON

I had to jump for it. Luckily, I was wearing my parachute, normally I don't bother, all those canvas and leather straps get in the way and the buckles are always catching on things. Anyway, if you're cruising below a thousand feet the bloody thing won't open before you hit the ground, so I usually wear a safety harness, like the ocean-going yachtsmen. As I was planning to fly higher than usual, using an upper wind to get to Edinburgh, I'd strapped on the old 'chute before I set off.

When the explosive charges severed the rear cables of the gondola, I'd clung onto the airship's steering wheel, then climbed onto the pedestal as the ship rose rapidly into the freezing air. *If I ever meet up with Lampeter again I won't hesitate.... I let him go, and this is how he rewards me.*

There was nothing I could do to control the ascent, so I jumped. I'd had no parachute training, although I'd read about landing with one's feet together and falling over or some such. My initial worry was that I'd become tangled in the loose ropes and rigging as I left my beloved 'Estella' to her spiralling journey up into the heavens. I fell free, and as the wind rushed past, my 'chute opened like a beautiful white blossom above me. I allowed myself a few moments to enjoy the view as the temperature slowly rose and I dangled down towards the ground.

***

Now I know what you're thinking.

'Why would a man, living towards the end of the twenty-first century be floating around in an airship, driven by a steam engine?' And you'd be right to ask this, as you sit there with your iPhones, your Internet, your central heating, your televisions and music players. The answer is, of course, that wanker Dr Martin Riley. He that invented the 'CleanBurn' system that drove the 'TrashBots' that litter the world like dead and rusting horseshoe crabs.

It all seemed like a good idea at the time, bots crawling around at all hours cleaning up after us, collecting trash and taking it back to their depots for sorting. Every city and municipality on the planet bought into the idea, and issued licenses to the franchisees. Sorting the plastics was the problem though. The bacterium *Ideonella sakaiensis* was originally found in a Japanese recycling plant, decades ago, but Dr Riley managed to 'improve' it. He came up with a bacterium that could rapidly digest plastic of all types, leaving a viscous hydrocarbon residue that could be recycled.

'But wouldn't a bacterium that digested plastic be a little dangerous, Dr Riley?' I hear you ask.

'Nothing to worry about, it can't breed outside our fermentation tanks, and it has a short life span, it's all perfectly safe. Ha, ha,' says the good doctor.

'So, no risk of them escaping and screwing up the whole world then? No chance, they'd start breeding and rapidly return us all to the steam age?' Wrong on all counts, Dr Riley.

You can guess the rest, here we are back in the Victorian age, a hundred and fifty years after the old Queen died. We have a much smaller population now.

'And the Government in Edinburgh?' you ask. Well, the Scots had the oil, didn't they? And although the sight of sailing boats making deliveries to oil platforms might seem anachronistic to you, to me it seems perfectly normal.

***

But in the meantime, I was about to make my first parachute landing a mile or two from where I set off. I arrived with a hell of a thump and lay for a while as my heart slowly stopped hammering and the trembling in my legs diminished. I stood up, folded my parachute and plodded back to the farmhouse, hoping to get help from the farmer's wife.

'Madam, the scrap value of my airship's boiler alone is worth more than your paltry smallholding.' I gave an all-encompassing gesture. Her ignoramus of a husband was probably arranging the sale of my wrecked boiler and engine as we spoke. She stood, hands on hips, a sullen and uncooperative expression on her face. To add insult to injury, my top hat was firmly wedged on the head of this squat and dumpy denizen of the Hertfordshire countryside.

‘Ye can ’ave the bike for the para-thingy,’ she said, pointing at my bundle.

I handed over my rumpled silk parachute, and she seemed to cheer up as she fingered the material, no doubt imagining all the uses she could put it to: the frilly underwear she could make, what an appalling thought.

I set off on the bone-shaking old bicycle, its tyres stuffed with grass or similar, and headed for the nearest town - Letchworth, as a matter of interest. The salesman at Ichneald Car Sales couldn’t have been more helpful, once I began to unstitch the hem of my coat and pile gold sovereigns on his desk.

‘You’d prefer a steam buggy to one of the two-stroke petrol jobs, Sir?’

‘I’m heading North and can’t guarantee petrol supplies on the way. With a steamer, I can forage for fuel as I go.’ We retired to the local hostelry, and he stood me a fine lunch while his mechanics fired up the boiler of my new acquisition, to raise steam for my journey.

I intend to make my way to the A1 carriageway and then on up to Glasgow on the A66. There’s a certain engineer up there who can’t wait to see these drawings and start work on the Ironclad warship. She’ll probably want to steam up the Thames in it and bombard the Houses of Parliament. She’s a fiery thing is Aileen, and God, how she hates the English.

And, by the way, I waited until Lampeter was asleep, and replaced the counterfeit plans in his coat pocket. I still have the originals. His clumsy substitution was far too obvious.

3 - FAMILY AFFAIRS

Harry Lampeter arrived at the old Royal Naval Observatory building to report to his boss, Ms Rigby. The Secret Intelligence Service had taken the building over after the Americans bombed the Vauxhall Cross site ten years before. There were those that said the bombing had been done with the agreement of the then SIS Chief, and wielder of the green pen, Brigadier Crisp.

The death toll had been quite shocking but it hadn't included Crisp, who was briefing the Prime Minister at Downing Street at the time of the attack. The Yanks explained it away as an accident but the CIA obviously didn't want any interference from SIS as they proceeded with the incorporation of the United Kingdom as the fifty-fourth State of the Union.

Harry clattered across the beautifully tiled floors of the Observatory. He ignored the marble busts of long-dead admirals and politicians, the brass and steel naval instruments and telescopes displayed in alcoves, the classical pediments and fluted columns. A uniformed guard stood at Ms Rigby's polished mahogany door. He knocked, turned the brass handle with a white-gloved hand and pushed the door open.

'Ms Rigby will see you immediately, Sir.'

Harry mock saluted and walked in. His boss was sitting behind her desk reading a report, she pretended not to notice him, but Harry wasn't to be intimidated by such puerile dominance tactics. He plunked himself down in the chair opposite and banged his cowboy-booted feet on top of her desk one after the other.

'All right, Ms Rigby? Have you missed me? Here's a present for you.' He chuckled as he tossed the Ironclad warship plans onto the desk. They rolled over and Ms R was forced to stop them before they fell to the floor. She turned her cropped head towards him scowling, inserted her monocle and unrolled the blueprints. She pulled out the main assembly drawing, discarded the rest, and held it flat on her desk. Running her finger down the parts list she stopped and peered closely for a moment.

'So, Lampeter, another fuckup. These are the wrong plans. These are the ones we wanted the Northerners to work from. You didn't manage to switch them after all.' She glared at him.

'I switched them rather elegantly, I thought, Ms R. At the point of Telford's gun, I might add.'

'Well, Telford must have switched them back,' she hissed. 'This drawing calls for the armour plating to be one and three-eighths of an inch thick. It should be thirteen-sixteenths of an inch.' She threw the plans back violently. It was Harry's turn to catch them this time. 'Take your skinny arse up to Glasgow, retrieve the originals and leave these in their place. Get it right this time, Lampeter. Think of the damage an Ironclad could do if they build one before we can. You're an idiot, Lampeter, now get out and get on with it.' Ms Rigby was shouting and red in the face by the end of her tirade. Her monocle had dropped out and was hanging by its black string, swinging pendulum-like across the front of her mannish jacket.

Harry grabbed the drawings, stood and turned to leave. As he opened the door he turned back. 'So, no chance of a blowjob then, Ms R?' He passed through, chuckling and, as he was closing the door behind him, he heard the sound of Ms R's heavy glass ashtray smashing into the other side. 'Probably her funny week,' he said to the uniformed functionary as he sauntered away down the echoing hallway.

***

An hour later Harry stepped from a steam omnibus outside a terrace of brick houses in Hackney. He walked down the steps to a basement flat. Ignoring the litter and smell of urine, he checked for the door key under a flowerpot containing a dead and withered hydrangea. It wasn't there, so he knocked. The door was answered by a young woman wearing a corset, high heels and a small bonnet trimmed with feathers and lace.

'Oh, hello, Harry, I was just trying this out, d'you like the hat?'

'I certainly do, I like the whole confection, Emma.' He followed her into the hall and through into the bedroom where she stood in front of a full-length mirror adjusting her headgear. Harry sat on the bed and watched her. 'I love the new tattoo,' he said as he looked at the slightly romanticised rendering of Emma's friend and lover Elsa Nielson, on her left buttock. The image was wearing a small top hat with a bejewelled, skeletal hand on the side and a flower in the hat band.

‘It cost an effing fortune and hurt like anything. It’s still sore now, but then it’s only been a few days.’

Lampeter stood and began to undress. ‘I’m knackered Emma, any chance of a quick one and a few hours kip?’

‘Only for you, you silver-tongued devil,’ she said archly, as she pulled back the covers and climbed in. ‘You watch out for the tat, I don’t want it smudged.’

Harry chopped two lines out on the glass top of the bedside cabinet. With a magician-like flourish, he produced an ivory snuff tube and offered it to Emma.

‘After you, Darling,’ he said.

***

Some hours later, Harry was pulling on his velvet bell bottoms. He pulled out a handkerchief and tried to rub off the ink stains on his left thigh. ‘Bollocks to it, it’ll wear off,’ he muttered as he pulled his trousers up.

Meanwhile, Emma was standing with her back to the mirror, half turned, examining her tattoo.

‘You’ve fucking smudged it, Harry.’ She was tearful, ‘I told you to be careful. You’re always doing things like this, you only care about yourself. You don’t give a fuck about anybody else.’

Harry put his arms around her and gently kissed her cheek. ‘I do care about you, Emma, I really do. Here, take this. I’m sure you can get it fixed.’ He handed her a thin bundle of white five-pound notes and stroked her shoulder. ‘Anyway, thanks for the bed and board,

Emma, say 'Hello' to your Mum from me. Tell her I'll call around when I can.'

She heard the door slam and Harry's footsteps as he climbed the steps up to the street, then he was gone. Emma sighed, then walked to the telephone to dial her friend Elsa. She looked at the fivers and ran a finger over the portrait of old President Trump on the top one. Elsa picked up.

'Hello love, it's me. Harry's just been over. I had a lovely surprise lined up for you and now he's gone and ruined it.' She wept softly.

'Don't upset yourself, Em, he's not worth it. I'll come straight over and you can tell me all about it.'

4 - THE BEAR AND PENGUIN

Harry walked along Chatsworth Road and noticed the US Army lorry in Millfields Park. Four GI's were playing cards at a collapsible table next to it, they didn't look up as he passed. A cable curved up from it to a tethered balloon, a few hundred feet overhead. There was an aluminium cabin hanging underneath, with an underslung turret. A pair of heavy machine guns projected from it. As Harry walked past the railings, the turret rotated around and its occupant brought the guns to bear on him. Harry waved a two-fingered salute and called up, 'I'm a rear gunner meself occasionally mate.' He jerked his hips back and forth, laughing. The guns continued to track him as he walked on down the road.

A few minutes later, Harry pushed through the doors into the Saloon Bar of the 'Bear and Penguin.' At a corner table, making a dog's breakfast out of rolling a cigarette, sat 'Shaky' Tom Fletcher. His hands stopped shaking as he looked up.

'Thanks very much, I'll have a Guinness please, Harry, since you ask.' Harry chuckled and ordered two pints at the bar, then walked over to Tom's table. Tom's hands were trembling again.

'Hello, Tom,' said Harry sitting down, he reached over, gently took the 'makings' from Tom and quickly finished rolling the cigarette, lit up, and took a grateful pull.

'I thought that was for me,' said Tom, his hands trembling on the table in front of him.

'Piss off, roll your own,' laughed Harry. He shrugged, then reached across the table for Tom's tobacco tin and rolled one for him. 'You should smoke proper cigarettes, Tom,' he said, 'it'd be much easier for you.'

'I don't like the taste of tailor-mades Harry, that's the trouble.'

'You're a man of the world, Tom, what's all this feet and inches stuff nowadays?' asked Harry.

'Oh, well, it's all part of the Government's "Americanisation Campaign" I suppose.' Their drinks arrived and they clinked glasses. 'Chin-chin,' said Tom.

'And another thing, why's this pub called 'The Bear and Penguin?' asked Harry.

'Somethink to do with the North and South Poles, I believe. Anyway Harry, to what do I owe this unexpected pleasure?'

'I've got a job for you, Tom.'

'Sorry, Harry, I have certain responsibilities to my customers.' He parted one side of his jacket to show a bunch of small, cloth, drawstring coke bags hanging around his neck. 'People are relying on me.' Harry tossed a bundle of white fivers on the table in front of him. It was thicker than the one he'd given to Emma. A second later the notes were gone, Tom's gaze had never left Harry's face. 'I see, and er, how can I help?'

'I need you to come up to Scotland with me and pick a few locks, Tom.'

***

Tom and Harry were astride the Norton, leathered up, they'd been travelling for several hours. As Harry drifted the bike around the Scotch Corner roundabout and on up the A66 towards Glasgow, he overtook a number of steam buggies. One of them was driven by Telford Stephenson but Harry didn't spot him as he wasn't wearing his trademark top hat.

***

Harry sat in a booth in the whisky bar of the 'Oran Mor' public house and sipped a dram of the Macallan.

His left hand was roving under the table. His companion, a young draughtsman from Govan Shipbuilders was sitting silently and very upright, a faraway look on his face. 'I never realised the accessibility a kilt gives,' said Harry, 'I must get one of my own, is there such a thing as a 'Lampeter' tartan, do you think?'

'I've really no idea, Mr Lampeter.'

'Now come on, Hamish, all I want to know is where they keep the drawings. Make a little plan, you ought to be good at that, being a draughtsman, just a simple sketch.' Harry placed a piece of paper and a pencil in front of him. 'Let me know when you've finished,' he said, as he ducked under the table and disappeared from view.

Hamish drew the paper towards him and tried to concentrate. 'I think you'll know when I'm finished, Mr Lampeter,' he muttered.

***

Earlier that afternoon, Telford Stephenson had arrived at the door of the design department at Govan Shipbuilders and walked through to Aileen Anderson's office. The sign proclaimed her 'Chief Mechanical Engineer'. Telford knocked and let himself in.

'Hello, darling,' he said as he laid a drawing tube on her desk.

'I've told you before, Telford, don't call me "darling". At the office, I'm Ms Anderson. It's hard enough dealing with the numpties that work here and call themselves "engineers" without them calling me "darling" behind my back.'

'Sorry, darling,' said Telford. Aileen sighed.

'Alright, what have you brought me?'

'Well, it's the drawings for the Ironclad class of warships the Southerners are going to manufacture. All the latest weaponry, triple expansion steam engines, built of wood but with steel cladding above and below the waterline. Actually, they look rather like those broken-down TrashBot things that one's always coming across. Sort of like tanks, with slits for the chaps to push their muskets through.'

'Don't talk dirty, Telford.'

'Sorry, Aileen.'

'Here, let me have a look at them.' Aileen cast an expert eye over the drawings while Telford pumped up the paraffin stove and made them both a cup of coffee. He sat quietly for a while, then walked out into the design area and rummaged around the drawing boards until he found a copy of 'The Scotsman.' Back in Aileen's office he sat and did the crossword. After about three-quarters of an hour, Aileen looked up.

'I've seen enough, there's nothing here we can't duplicate. It'll take a year to build the first one, six months to build the second, as we'll have made all the templates and patterns'

She counter-rolled the drawings to flatten them, laid them in the top drawer of her drawing chest and spun the combination lock. Telford stood, looking undecided, as Aileen bustled into her coat and gathered her things. 'Right, Telford, let's go back to my place and you can wine, dine and have a lovely conversation with me.'

Telford brightened up and followed her out of the door.

5 - THE STONE OF DESTINY

Telford and Aileen arrived at her flat in Maryhill. They took off their coats and retired to the lounge, Aileen lit the gas fire.

‘It doesn’t get much better than this Telford, a takeaway and a bottle of fizz. God, I do love haggis pakora.’ They ate their meal and then snuggled on the sofa.

‘It’s been a while since we’ve er, been together, Aileen, what with me being on my mission down south. I could sleep on the sofa if you like.’

‘Don’t be silly, Telford, a woman has needs too.’ She led him to the bedroom. They kissed frantically, helped remove each other’s clothes and climbed into bed.

‘Say it Telford, say it for me,’ whispered Aileen, as they lay in each other’s arms.

‘Oh, thou wee and timorous beastie...’

‘No, Telford, no, I want “Tam o’Shanter”.’

‘Oh, alright, erm, let me see:

When the peddler people leave the street,

And thirsty neighbours, neighbours meet,

As market days are wearing late,’

‘Yes, Telford, yes,’ said Aileen. ‘I love hearing you reciting Burns in that whiney English accent of yours.’

‘The legacy of a private education I’m afraid, old thing. The Royal Hospital Naval Academy has a lot to answer for. Particularly my form teacher, Mr Sedgewick. The thrashings he gave me if I ever lapsed into Scottish vernacular, I was 11 years old, only a young shaver,' he sighed. Aileen shook his shoulder. They continued making love until he'd finished the poem. Aileen gasped and lay back.

'Would you like me to recite something else, darling?'

'No, Telford, that was wonderful. What we need now is some inspirational music. Put 'Flower of Scotland' on the gramophone, and we'll see what we can do for *you*.'

'Oh, not to worry, darling, I'm quite tired, and rather full of Chicken Korma, if the truth be told. Would you like me to rub your back?'

***

Dressed in their leathers again, Harry and 'Shaky' Tom stood in a cobbled street at a side entrance to the Govan Shipbuilders drawing office. Tom was concentrating on picking the lock. His hands didn't shake as long as he was talking, so he kept up a monologue as he worked. Harry stood at his side, illuminating the lock with the smoky flame of a carbide lantern and watching the street, but managing to look nonchalant as he did so. He had a cardboard tube under one arm.

'And another thing, Harry, kilts was invented by an Englishman called Thomas Rawlinson in the 18th century. Not a lot of Scottish people know that,' said Tom.

'Nor would want to. How do *you* know that?' asked Harry;

'I'm in the pub quiz team at the Bear and Penguin, I know lots of things.' There was a click and Tom pushed the door open. His hands began to shake again. Harry followed him in, shut the door and walked ahead, reading the floorplan the young draughtsman had drawn for him by the hissing yellow light of his lamp. They moved up a flight of stairs and along a corridor to the drawing office. The door was locked. Tom stepped forward holding his trembling lock pick.

'And all this foreign food, I mean, the trouble is you don't have to cut it up, Harry. Curry and rice, chow mein, macaroni, you just shovel it in and, before you know it, the meal's over. Give me meat and two veg with a knife and fork, every time.' He pushed the door open and Harry led the way to Aileen's small office. Tom managed to get his pick into place then read the sign on the door. He began to work. 'Honestly, Harry, how can a *girl* be a mechanical engineer? I mean, it stands to reason, it's a bloke's game, innit.' There was another click, the door opened, and they walked into Aileen's office.

'It says here that there's a large cabinet with a combination lock on it,' said Harry, looking at the plan again. 'Ah, there it is.'

Tom pulled a stethoscope out of his pocket, inserted the earpieces and held the chestpiece to the cabinet. Grimacing, he began to slowly rotate the dial on the drawing cabinet back and forth. 'You asked about the name of the pub, the "Bear and Penguin." Well, polar bears live at the south pole and penguins live at the north pole.'

'So, they're "Poles apart" then,' chuckled Harry.

Tom ignored the interruption and continued. 'So polar bears should never be in the company of penguins, not in the natural course of events.' He continued to work on the lock.

‘So, the pub’s name is an attempt at surrealistic humour, then?’ asked Harry.

‘Either that or unadulterated ignorance. Got you, you little bastard. There you are, Harry.’ He stepped back. ‘I don’t suppose you could roll me another ciggie?’

Harry pulled out the top drawer and saw the Ironclad plans in plain view. ‘Bingo, first time lucky.’ He lifted them out, substituted the fakes, rolled up the originals and dropped them into the empty cardboard tube. ‘Right, that’s it, Tom. Goodbye Caledonia, and back to civilisation.’ They retraced their steps, locking up as they went.

‘That’s a shame, Harry, I was just getting used to the accent, I can nearly understand people now,’ said Tom.

The Norton was in the side street where they’d left it. Harry kicked it into life and minutes later they were roaring through Renfrew on the way to the old M74 and the long run down to London.

***

Next morning, Aileen and Telford sat at breakfast. Telford had three boiled eggs in front of him, all of which he’d decapitated and examined. ‘I’ve always been a bit funny about boiled eggs, I like a soft yolk but I can’t stand the white being runny’ makes me go all shivery,’ Aileen had cooked the three eggs for two minutes, two and a half minutes, and three minutes, respectively. Telford had chosen to eat the one on his right.

‘It all depends on the size, Telford, it’s quite simple, the bigger they are, the longer they take.’

'I'm sure you're right, darling, and it's very nice of you to go to this trouble for me. We ought to get back to the shipyard as soon as possible, you never know, Lampeter might have another go at switching the plans if he realises, we've still got the originals.'

'Don't worry, Telford, they're all safely locked away. I'm not going to let those Sassenach bastards pull the wool over *my* eyes.'

'You know, Aileen, I realise we're on opposite sides to them, but I've never really understood why you hate the English so much.'

'They stole the Stone of Scone, the Stone of Destiny, the most ancient symbol of Scottish monarchy and independence,' said Aileen.

'But that was in 1296, nearly a thousand years ago,' said Telford, 'and they gave it back in the end.'

'Aye, they gave it back, but it was broken,' said Aileen, her voice rising.

'Still, it's a long time to hold a grudge, darling.'

6 - TURNABOUT'S FAIR PLAY

Telford and Aileen pedalled through the, dank, deserted streets of Glasgow, north towards the shipyard. Having spent time in London, Telford barely noticed the smell of smoke, sewage, horse dung and garbage. They parked and locked the tandem at the entrance to the offices. The design area was empty as they walked through and unlocked Aileen's office. Telford lit and pumped the brass paraffin stove to boil the kettle. Aileen opened her cabinet, lifted out the top drawing and began scrutinising it. After a few minutes, she paused.

'It looks as if you were right, Telford, somebody's switched these drawings, the armour plating is specified at nearly three-quarters of an inch thicker than it was yesterday. It would make the ship top heavy, it would turn turtle. Just what they'd like to see happen.'

'It's lucky you had such a good look at them yesterday.' He placed a cup of tea and a plate of biscuits on her desk. 'Gingernuts, darling, the best for dunking.'

Aileen nodded and got busy with her correcting fluid and draughting pen. Telford looked over her shoulder. 'Right,' she said after a few minutes, 'these can go to the repro department and then I'll distribute them.'

'I really don't like the look of these Ironclad things. They remind me of over-turned wheelbarrows,' said Telford.

'If you talk to anybody in the Government, just keep your opinions to yourself,' said Aileen. 'Nobody wants to be told they have an ugly baby, Telford.'

***

Harry and Tom had ridden south all night with only a few short breaks. They parked the Norton outside the 'Bear and Penguin.' Harry knew Tom had a rented room somewhere, but he seemed to spend his life at the pub. Rosie, the landlady, was sweeping the step as they arrived.

'Hello, Tom, Harry, if you want a drink, you've come to the right place.' She laughed her forty-a-day laugh and then lapsed into a fit of coughing. Harry patted her on the back.

'Not for me, Rosie, I could do with a coffee though.'

They went inside and Harry was struck by the sad atmosphere of an empty pub in the morning. The coal fire had just been lit and wasn't throwing out any heat. The air smelled of yeast, sweat and stale tobacco smoke. The low plaster ceiling was cracked, yellowed and water-stained. In the 'artists corner,' the ceiling had been covered in pencil drawings of all sorts: animals, girls, politicians. Copper pennies had been pushed into the cracks in the beams for good luck.

'Pint of Guinness for me,' said Tom as he sat down at his usual table. He handed Harry his tobacco tin. 'You might roll me a few spares, Harry.'

‘I’m fed up with rolling your cigarettes, what are you going to do when I’m not here?’

Tom sighed and picked up the tin. ‘These Scotsmen who sound like Englishmen, I mean, it shouldn’t be allowed. They look the same as us when they’re wearing trousers, they could be spying on us, they should have to wear a badge or something.’ He just had time to roll a cigarette during his tirade. He fell silent, lit up despite his renewed shakes, and stared moodily into the distance.

Tom’s words reminded Harry of his old friend, Telford, the English-sounding Scotsman. He knew he’d escaped from his doomed airship because the Ironclad plans had been delivered to Glasgow. Harry hoped he didn’t hold a grudge. *After all, all’s fair in love and war*, he thought.

‘Okay, Tom, got to go. See you soon, I hope. Bye, Rosie.’ He walked towards the door. Tom waved languidly and took a sip of his frothy stout.

‘See ya, Harry, look after yourself.’

***

Harry had been ushered into Ms Rigby’s office, there were no longer any seats, except the one she was occupying, so Harry had no choice but to stand. He laid the roll of drawings on her desk. She kept him waiting for several minutes as she leafed through them.

Looking up, she removed her monocle. ‘We won’t be renewing your contract, Lampeter, your relationship with SIS is over. You’re going to have to get a job and work for a living, like the rest of us.' Her voice was flat, her face expressionless.

'I've never done a day's work in my life, Ms R, as you well know,' said Harry.

'I expect you'll team up with that half-wit friend of yours, Thomas Fletcher. What was it he did before he started dealing in drugs?' she asked.

'He was a brain surgeon, I believe. You know, Ms Rigby, that red lipstick you wear does something for me. I can't stop thinking about it, it haunts my fantasies, you on your knees...' Harry was moving towards the door.

'Get out, Lampeter, get out now or I'll....' She wrenched open the top drawer of her desk and lifted out a black revolver, pointed it up at the ceiling, and fired a deafening shot. 'GET OUT,' she screamed. Before Harry could reach the door, it was thrown open as the guard burst into the room.

'I can see we're going to have to work very hard at this relationship, Ms R,' said Harry seriously as he left. As he walked down the corridor, he could hear the guard asking her to put the gun down.

'Temper, temper,' chuckled Harry as he sauntered away. He walked down the steps at the front of the building and stood in the wintry morning, wondering what to do next. He could go to his flat for a rest, or around to Emma's for some 'company,' or back to the Bear and Penguin for a drink. He took a deep breath of the frosty air. A nice big breakfast was called for, he decided to visit his Club.

He left the Norton in the secure car park at the Observatory. A pedal rickshaw was passing, and he flagged it down, Harry climbed in and sat back to enjoy the journey as they set off for the Travellers Club in Pall Mall. The Americans had brought in more surveillance balloons with their underslung rotating turrets and machine guns; he caught the occasional reflection from the observers' binoculars as they swept the city, looking for targets. Tower Bridge was still standing, along with the aerial walkway that joined the towers, but the suspension bridges that led up to them on either side were twisted wreckage, lying rusting in the stinking waters of the River Thames, and occupied by rows of seagulls. They passed what remained of the Shard, a smoke-blackened ruin. *The Yanks have certainly had their fun*, thought Harry.

The rickshaw rattled over the still intact Golden Jubilee bridge, crossed the Mall and stopped outside the Travellers Club. Harry paid the driver and stood looking up for a moment, admiring the club's Renaissance architecture. A US Air Force biplane flew over, a rare sight. Harry went inside, made his way to the Coffee Room and took a corner table. He couldn't remember when he'd eaten last.

7 – BRIGADIER CRISP

Harry was enjoying a mixed grill when a stranger approached his table and coughed apologetically. 'Sorry to bother you, old chap, but I, er, have a proposition for you. Would you mind awfully if I sit down?' Harry waved his fork in invitation then loaded it with a juicy piece of steak and thrust it into his mouth. He liked the knee britches, green woolly stockings and polished brown brogues; the large tweedy figure manoeuvred its bulk into the chair opposite.

'The name's Crisp, Brigadier Crisp, used to be in the same game as yourself, still am, actually, but, er, freelance now, not working for His Majesty's Government any more. Had a disagreement, parting of the ways, irreconcilable differences, so to speak. Heard you might be available for an enterprise that's come my way.'

'I know you, Brigadier, seen your picture on the corridor at the Observatory, previous heads of SIS and all that. Yours is covered in spit. Probably to do with the Yanks attacking the old building at Vauxhall Cross and killing most of the workforce, while you were elsewhere.'

'Yes, yes, water under the bridge, Lampeter, long time ago, ancient history. Can we have a chat about the Scots? You've recently come down from Edinburgh, I believe.'

Despite his nonchalant manner, Harry was impressed by how up-to-date Crisp's intelligence was, he decided the Brigadier must still have contacts in SIS. 'Yes, Brigadier, that's right, I'm just back. How can I help? What's the caper?'

'I'm working for the Cousins now, you understand. The head of their CIA's been in touch, chap called Wilson, nasty piece of work, ex-special forces, wears a bootlace tie and one of those silver and turquoise woggle things that the Yanks like. And you can't trust a man who wears short-sleeved shirts, anathema, beyond the pale. Fellow was wearing a shoulder holster too, looked like a bloody gangster.'

'So, putting his appalling dress sense to one side, what was his proposition?' asked Harry

The Brigadier leaned forward and whispered. 'The Americans don't approve of the north-south divide: they plan to turn the whole of the mainland of Great Britain into their fifty-fourth state. Don't want to deal with two governments, two legal systems: it would be much simpler in terms of the bureaucracy, laws, all that sort of thing, if there was no Scottish Government. Once they've taken us under their wing, they intend to move on to the island of Ireland, unify it, and make it the fifty-fifth state.'

Harry had to swallow quickly before he burst into laughter. 'What could possibly go wrong with that plan, Brigadier? Unify the Prods and the Micks? That'll be the day.' He paused, 'I will await the result with interest,' he said soberly and took another mouthful of food. 'So, how do I fit into this Grand Plan?' he asked.

'Well, you know how it is with our transatlantic cousins, shoot first and see if there's anybody left alive to ask questions afterwards.

They basically want us to subdue Edinburgh, seat of the Scottish Government and all that.'

'And how do they propose we do that?' asked Harry.

'Well, a tactical nuke, old boy. Just a small one, you understand. Cause enough collateral damage to make them see sense.'

'I didn't think we had that technology any more, Brigadier, not since Dr Riley's plastic eating microbes,' said Harry, taking a sip of coffee.

'Apparently, the Yanks have all sorts of stuff they keep in a bug-free bunker in the Rocky Mountains or somewhere. Once they bring the bomb out, they can only guarantee its integrity for a few weeks, what with the microbes eating all the electrics, and all.'

'So, they'll ship it over on a steamer, deliver it to us, and we'll arrange placement?' asked Harry.

'That's right, Lampeter, that's exactly right,' the Brigadier was red in the face and becoming excitable. 'I mean, ours not to reason why and all that, job to do, just need to get on with it. Serious money in it, name your own price, within reasonable limits. So, will you do it then, Lampeter?' Brigadier Crisp sat back and mopped his sweat filmed brow with a large white handkerchief.

'I most certainly will, Brigadier,' said Harry as he placed his knife and fork on his now empty plate, and pushed his chair back. 'Anything for a laugh.' He began to chuckle, the Brigadier joined in. Their chuckles became belly laughs and Harry slapped the table. Several of the staff and the few early diners at the other tables looked across at them.

'This calls for champagne,' said the Brigadier, summoning the maitre'd. 'A toast, a toast to Confederation with our American allies.'

***

One bottle of champagne and a couple of large brandies later, Harry left the Club and took an omnibus north to Hackney. He arrived at Emma's flat, her friend Elsa Nielson answered the door.

'Hello, Harry, how are you?' she asked.

Harry stepped inside, 'I was passing and thought I'd call in for a cup of tea.'

'Come through, Harry, Emma's in the bedroom.'

Harry saw that Emma was standing in front of the mirror as usual, but naked this time, except for the shoes and the hat she'd been wearing on his previous visit.

'Hello, Emma,' said Harry. 'Did you get that tattoo fixed?'

'I did, Harry, thanks. It was only a bit of ink leaking, no harm done, I forgive you. You look knackered, H, are you overdoing things again? We were going to get our heads down for a few hours, want to join us?' She kicked off her shoes, placed her hat on the dressing table and climbed into bed.

Elsa slid out of her frock and laid it over a chair. 'We're just back from a party at the Archbishop's. We were putting on a show for him and his guests.'

She got into the other side of the bed.

'Come on, Harry,' said Elsa, patting the mattress between her and Emma, 'you can be the meat in our sandwich.'

'Okay,' said Harry as he took off his jacket, 'but no biting, girls.'

'Maybe just a little nibble, here and there,' said Emma. The girls pulled the covers over their heads, giggling.

8 – IN THE BOTANIC GARDENS

Telford's contact with the Scottish Secret Intelligence Service was Owen Turrell, an experienced agent handler, who put the welfare of his joes first, wherever operational constraints allowed. Telford was an 'occasional,' employed casually. They met in the ancient glass house of the Botanic Gardens in the park at the West End of Glasgow. Telford always enjoyed visiting the Gardens, he loved the warm, damp atmosphere, the mossy smells, the exotic plants, the white marble statues. He and Owen went through the pantomime of old chums bumping into each other, under the main glass rotunda. Having exclaimed their surprise at the lucky coincidence, they retired to the tearooms in the garden of the former Curator's house. The weather was warm enough to sit outside and avoid potential eavesdroppers. Both men wore kilts although neither of them wore clan tartans. Owen's was a grey Prince of Wales check and Telford's a tasteful Paisley.

'You've done well, Telford,' said Owen, quietly. 'The Tech Services people have received their copy of the Ironclad plans from Aileen Anderson.'

'What do you think will happen next?' asked Telford.

'That's up to the Government, but if they've any sense, they'll start building an Ironclad immediately. It's an arms race, and we can't let the English get the jump on us.' He laughed, 'Aileen has added a note about steaming up the Thames and pulverising the Palace of Westminster. I don't suppose it'll come to that though. Anyway, more urgently, I've another job for you. Normally, it would be above your pay grade, but you're in a privileged position because you know this character, Harry Lampeter.'

'Know him? We're intimately acquainted, he tried to kill me a few days ago.'

'Well, this could be the making of you, Telford, your chance of a permanent contract with SSIS, even with your plummy accent and no calf muscles.'

***

'How did your meeting go?' asked Aileen when she got back to the flat that evening.

'I'm not supposed to talk about it.' Telford was sitting in an armchair, glass in hand. Aileen noticed that his speech was slightly slurred and the bottle of Grant's, which stood on the coffee table next to him, was half empty.

She sat opposite him and saw he'd been crying. 'What's the matter, Telford, you can tell me, we're on the same side, my love.'

Telford got up, found a second glass and poured a drink for Aileen. He stood, bottle in hand, undecided, then blurted, 'It's that fucking Harry Lampeter again. He's going to blow up Edinburgh with an atom bomb.'

Just for a moment, Aileen, who had been born and raised in Glasgow, wondered if this would be an altogether bad thing. The

Edinbuggers were such a self-important lot, with their snooty accents and haughtiness. Just because the Scottish Parliament was in Edinburgh, they thought they were more important than the rest of the country. She dismissed the thought, a united front against the 'Auld Enemy' in the south was called for. Internecine grudges could wait.

Telford sat down in the chair again and held his head in his hands. 'SSIS want me to kill him,' he said. 'We went to school together, we used to be friends.'

Aileen leaned over and put an arm around his shoulders. 'There, there, Telford, is this the same man that blew up your dirigible? I'm sure he deserves your enmity, but tell me about the bomb. Where would he get such a thing?'

Telford told Aileen of the plan to blow up the Scottish Parliament.

'But how do SSIS know all this? Surely, the English would keep it under wraps, the first we'd hear of it would be the explosion.'

'Well it's not so much the English as the Americans, they're the ones who're employing Lampeter. I can only assume there's a double agent, a mole in SIS. My handler hinted that King George knows about it, too.'

'King George?' said Aileen, shocked.

'He's the only political figure who still spans the north-south divide, he's still King of both countries. He wouldn't let the Yanks blow up Edinburgh, not if he could do anything to prevent it.'

***

Harry stood on the shingle beach at Landgard Point watching the 'USS Hillary Clinton' arrive at Felixstowe docks. Its mission was to bring the bomb to Suffolk, US Marines would transport it to their headquarters at Martlesham, the old UK Government surveillance site ten miles away, and he'd take things on from there. Harry walked back to the road and kicked the Norton into life, it was time to fetch Tom.

***

'It's not very big,' said Tom, 'not considering its destructive potential.'

'The best things come in small packages,' drawled Colonel Wilson, the CIA chief. Somehow, he reminded Harry of an old movie star called Clint Eastwood, the same rangy, almost haggard look, the same slight swagger. He wore a grey wool jacket but Harry noticed the bulge under his left armpit. *Probably compensating for the size of his prick*, he thought.

The three were standing in a garage area at the Martlesham base, a dozen blank-faced Marine guards wearing camouflage fatigues and forage caps guarded the perimeter. *And with enough armament to take Scotland by themselves*, thought Harry. The object of interest was a grey metal box not much bigger than an overnight case, placed in a trailer attached to the back of Harry's motorcycle.

'It's a modified warhead from an old multiple re-entry vehicle,' said the Colonel. 'The yield is equivalent to about a thousand tons of TNT, plenty enough to flatten the Holyrood area of Edinburgh.' He pronounced it *Edinburrow*. 'Might even re-awaken the volcano the city's built on.' He chuckled, ran his finger over the top of the box and gestured to a figure wearing fatigues, who stood by the door. 'Sergeant Harbaugh here will show you how to arm it.'

'You're convinced this is the right thing to do then, Colonel?' asked Harry.

'Sometimes wrong, never hesitant,' said the Colonel, he winked and gently punched Harry's shoulder. 'Best of luck, Lampeter, bring me back a haggis, I've always wondered what they look like.' He turned on his heel and walked away briskly.

Harry looked at the trailer attached to his beloved bike. 'This'll affect the Norton's handling,' he complained.

'Perhaps you ought to drive a little slower than usual, considering the cargo,' said Tom. 'Personally, I'll be too nervous even to fart near it, in case it goes off.'

The Sergeant stepped between them, holding the key she wore on a lanyard around her neck, she unlocked the box and lifted the lid.

'Right,' said Harry, 'show us where to light the blue touch paper, Sergeant.

9 - THE WATER OF LEITH

Harry and Tom had rented a cottage in Rosyth, just North of Edinburgh. Tom sat at the dining table rolling himself a cigarette and looking across the front garden to the farmyard on the opposite side of the road.

'I love this part of the world, Harry,' he said. 'Probably the romantic old asbestos farm buildings, all covered in moss and lichen. I expect they've all got preservation orders on them.' He licked the glued edge of the cigarette paper. 'You know, Harry, I always thought Water of Leith was something you add to single malt whiskey but it turns out it's a river in the city.'

He finished making the roll-up and began shaking again, fumbling with his brass lighter. Harry had been staring into the middle-distance, he shook himself, reached across for the lighter and flicked it into life. Tom lit up and took a deep pull.

'I think you're getting mixed up with Malvern Water, Tom.'

'Where's that then, Harry?' Lampeter shrugged. Tom continued. 'So, Harry, blowing up Edinburgh with an atom bomb, seems a little extreme, even for you.'

Harry grimaced. 'You're right, Tom, we can't do it. They may be a bunch of kilt-wearing caber-tossers but they don't deserve that. I've been wondering how we can still get the other half of the money without doing the job.'

'I doubt if we can, Harry,' said Tom. 'I mean, either we do it or we don't, there's no in between where tactical nuclear weapons are concerned. You either get a big bang or none at all.' He tried to take another pull but his cigarette had gone out.'

'Yes, I guess we'd better ditch the bomb and cut our losses. We'll tell the Yanks we placed it and armed it, but it was a dud, we did our best, it wasn't our fault. We can blame Martin Riley and his bacteria.'

'Tailor-made cigarettes have a lot of saltpetre in them,' said Tom, reaching for his lighter. 'That's why they never go out even if you leave them in the ashtray. Roll-ups are much healthier, fewer additives, just the pure tobacco.' He'd managed to light up. 'What do you propose doing with it?' He nodded towards the grey metal box on the floor near their feet. 'I don't fancy taking it back to Suffolk, you know what the Yanks are like, they might use it on London or something'

'We'll drop it off the Queensferry Bridge and into the Firth of Forth on our way home,' said Harry.

'And that's another thing, I always get mixed up with the Firth of Forth and the Forth of Firth. Why do they have to have such funny names up here?'

Harry ignored him. 'There's no time like the present, let's get it over with. It's your turn to drive.'

'Can't it wait, Harry, the rain's pissing down out there?'

'If we wait for the rain to stop in Scotland, we might be here for a week, come on, let's do it, then we can get back to the Smoke.'

***

The Queensferry Bridge was a windswept rusting hulk, the cables frayed and close to parting in places, the rain-washed decking brown and flaking. Dr Riley's bacteria had eaten the paint and left the steel exposed to the ravages of the atmosphere. Soon, the bridge would collapse, and only the three concrete support towers would be left standing. The depressing lack of maintenance was repeated in the decrepit old Forth Bridge that ran parallel to it. Parts had fallen off into the Firth, the only thing holding it up was faith, hope and good old Victorian over-engineering. This universal rusting of steel structures made for a gloomy and dystopian environment, and those erected closest to saltwater suffered the most.

Tom stopped the bike part way over the Bridge and kept the engine ticking over while Harry stepped off. He lifted the bomb out of the trailer and placed it on the parapet. There were a variety of other vehicles passing from both directions, a steam buggy stopped about twenty-five yards behind them. Telford Stephenson stepped out of the passenger's side, he pulled a revolver from each of the pockets of his waxed cotton riding coat and pointed them at Harry.

'Don't move, Lampeter,' he shouted through the wind and rain. 'We've been watching you ever since you crossed the border. I thought you were going to blow up Holyrood. What made you change your target? No, don't bother answering, I don't really care.' He began blasting, somewhat inexpertly, with both guns, in Harry's direction.

Harry dived over the edge of the parapet, taking the bomb with him, and began the long fall towards the cold, black waters below. Tom roared off in the direction of Edinburgh.

Telford looked over the edge as the falling figure splashed into the water. 'Good bye old friend,' he muttered, his tears lost among the raindrops spattering his face.

***

'How did it go, Telford?' asked Aileen, when he arrived back at the flat hours later. 'Did you arrest Lampeter or did you have to shoot him?' She stared, unblinking, holding his wet coat, before hanging it up.

'I think I winged him, but the fall will have killed him.'

'What fall, Telford?' she asked.

***

Shaky Tom found Harry lying unconscious on a small beach on the Edinburgh side of the Firth. He dragged him to the trailer, manhandled him into it, then headed south. When he was safely clear of Edinburgh and out into the countryside, he pulled off the road and made Harry as comfortable as he could. Fortunately, none of Telford's bullets had hit him. Tom drove for Carlisle as fast as he could and checked Harry into the hospital there, less than two hours later.

***

The grey metal box had smashed into the waters of the Firth of Forth beside Harry and sunk into its depths, even as the *Ideonella* bacteria had begun eating its plastic components. The current rolled it gently out into the North Sea where it eventually sank harmlessly into the mud, and began a slow and uneventful decomposition.

***

Three weeks later, Harry, Emma and Elsa Nielson caused a stir as they entered the Bear and Penguin. The girls were dressed to the nines with feathered bonnets, high heels and calf-length dresses. Harry wore a dark velvet suit, silk shirt and fedora. The twenty or so regulars raised a cheer, both at the return of Harry after his convalescence, and also the hope of a round of free drinks. The three joined Tom at his corner table.

'Hello, Harry, you look well. Emma and Elsa been looking after you, have they?' Tom winked and pushed his tobacco tin towards Harry, Harry pushed it towards Emma, she smiled, opened it and began to roll a cigarette for Tom.

'They've been keeping me warm, Tom, I'll say that for them.'

'And the Yanks, Harry, what about them?'

'It seems Colonel Wilson didn't have presidential approval for his plan. Apparently, there've been some telegraphic exchanges between the White House and Windsor Castle. The upshot is that the Colonel is no longer head of the CIA, and the grateful new director, with my promise of our discretion, has coughed up the rest of the money. Here's your share.' Harry tossed a thick bundle of notes onto the table in front of Tom.

Emma lit up and placed the roll-up in Tom's mouth. 'It looks like it's your round then, Tom,' she said. But Tom had already spirited the money away and was shaking again, this time, partly at least with laughter.

10 - A PROMENADE AT SOUTHWOLD

A year later

Telford was sitting at his table writing a letter to Aileen when the cell door opened. He looked up, 'Hello, Harry, I thought you'd turn up eventually,' he said, as his erstwhile schoolmate walked in.

'Been here long Tellers?' asked Harry, looking around at the whitewashed walls, the single gas lamp and the riveted steel door.

'Twenty-seven days, Harry, ever since I was captured at Southwold. I nearly got away with it, Aileen and I were the only members of the crew not in uniform.'

'But you were wearing a kilt, Telford, it's a bit of a giveaway in Suffolk.' Harry sat on the iron-framed bed, then lay back with his hands behind his head and closed his eyes. 'What's the story then, tell me all about it.'

'Well, Aileen wangled us berths on the SSS Revenge's maiden voyage. The sea trials had gone well, although the Captain said she'd wallowed a little in a heavy swell. Whatever that means. Anyway, we steamed out of Glasgow, up through the Caledonian Canal and then turned south. We stopped at Edinburgh to take on supplies, dignitaries came aboard, there were parties, photographers, stories in the papers. That was probably our undoing. We continued south down the east coast. The plan was to steam up the Thames, fire a few salvoes at the Houses of Parliament to put the wind up the English Government, and then steam back, show of strength and all that. Aileen was so excited she didn't sleep for three days. I think she was hoping to fire a round herself.'

'So, what went wrong?' asked Harry.

'Well, it was the bloody Yanks, wasn't it?' said Telford. 'They only bloody torpedoed us in Sole Bay, off Southwold in Suffolk. It wasn't much of a torpedo, probably clockwork or something, but it made quite a bang and we started taking in water through a hole in the stern. The bilge pumps couldn't keep up, the boat was heavy with all that iron plating on it, so the Captain decided to beach her. It was a race against time, we put on full steam straight towards the shore. The holidaymakers didn't know what to do, probably thought it was a stunt. Anyway, somebody must have telegraphed the militia, because by the time we reached the shallows and abandoned ship there were about twenty of them waiting for us. You can't put up much of a fight when you're waist deep in water and looking up the gun barrels of a squad of redcoats.'

'So, they arrested you?' asked Harry. He sat up, pulled a hip flask from his coat pocket and poured a large shot into Telford's tin mug.

'I say, Harry, you are a gent,' said Telford. 'Slangevar, old chap,' he said as he downed it. Harry poured him another. 'Sorry Harry, it's been a while, I'll sip this one.'

'So, there you are, wading ashore with Aileen on your arm, then what happened?'

'Well, as I said before, we nearly got away with it. We were both in civvies and some of the crowd had waded out to get a better look, so we sort of mixed in with them while the militia were concentrating on the chaps in uniform. We came ashore, actually, I bought us both an ice cream cone at a kiosk on the promenade to help us blend in. Bloody good ice cream it was, too, but as you said the kilt gave me away.'

'You should have taken it off, Telford, nobody would have noticed you in your pants at the seaside.'

'Afraid I wasn't wearing any, Harry, tradition and all that. Anyway, I told Aileen to leave me, she walked to the railway station and made her way back to Scotland over the next couple of days. She had a few sticky moments, but you English aren't big on security and identity papers and the border's pretty porous in places.'

'I'm glad she got home safe, Telford, she sounds like a gutsy sort of girl, just what you need.'

'Anyway, that's the story, I'm awaiting trial as a spy and can expect to be found guilty. I'll be executed at some unspecified time in the future. The rest of the chaps will be alright, as they were in uniform the Geneva Convention applies. They'll probably be exchanged and sent home in a few months, that seems to be the way it works. Meantime, I haven't heard a peep out of my employers, the Scottish Secret Intelligence Service.'

'Who was it said that "Military Intelligence" is a contradiction in terms?' asked Harry. He stood up and began removing his clothes.

'I say, Harry,' said Telford. 'Aren't we a bit too old for that sort of thing, we're supposed to have grown out of it?'

‘Shut up and put this on.’ Harry pulled a dark wig out of his pocket and threw it to Telford. ‘We’ll exchange clothes and you can piss off back over the border. Tom’s waiting outside with the Norton.’

Harry sat at the writing desk wearing his friend’s kilt and linen shirt, he’d tucked his hair into Telford’s tam-o'-shanter, and sat with his head in his hands as if upset. Dressed in Harry’s velvet suit and long-haired wig, Telford banged on the cell door and stood with his back to it as the guard entered.

‘I’m sorry I can’t help you, Telford,’ said Telford to his supposed self, using his best estuary accent. He walked past the guard and out of the cell.

***

Harry gave Telford twenty-four hours, and then declared himself to the guards, but nobody seemed to care much who occupied the cell, as long as they had somebody under lock and key. Two days passed before a guard came and escorted Harry, in handcuffs, to the visitation room. Only the centremost desk was occupied. The guard pushed Harry into the chair opposite Ms Rigby and stood behind him.

‘Hello, Ms R,’ said Harry. ‘Come to bail me out, have you?’

‘If I had my way, Lampeter, I’d leave you here to rot at the King’s pleasure.’ She was wearing her usual mannish grey suit, a white shirt and regimental tie, her hair was as short as ever. ‘That bloody man Crisp is back in the driving seat at SIS. The Yanks have been interfering again. You seem to be his blue-eyed boy, he won’t have a word said against you. He’s got another job for you, in Ireland this time, I'll be interested to see what sort of a balls-up you make of it. How they can still want you after you lost their precious atom bomb, I don't know. You realise it would have gone off as soon as you tried to set the timer. You're lucky to be here, by rights you should be a cloud of radioactive molecules dissipating into the atmosphere high above Scotland. Another thing I don't understand is why you helped Telford Stephenson escape. After all, according to your statement, he tried to kill you on the Queensferry Bridge.'

'I said he fired at me, Ms Rigby, but Telford is a crack shot, he won a silver medal in the schools pistol shooting championships, back in the day. He missed me on purpose, gave me the opportunity to jump and take my chances in the water. I couldn't let you bastards kill him, I couldn't see him die at the end of a rope, it's not civilised.'

'He's a spy, he knew the risks he was taking,' she hissed.

'Come on Ms R,' said Harry. 'It's all a laugh, it's all a game. You couldn't give me a hand job under the table, for old times' sake, could you? I've been on my own for days.'

Ms Rigby stood and gathered her things. 'Fuck off, Lampeter, you can make your own way back to London.' She stormed out of the room trying to knock the bolted down tables and chairs aside. The guard came over and unlocked Harry's cuffs. They both watched Ms Rigby try to slam the door, as she left, but it had a spring closer. Harry looked at the guard.

'Always worth a try, don't you think?'

'You're free to go, Mr Lampeter,' said the guard evenly. 'Follow me and we'll collect your things.'

***

That evening, in Glasgow, Telford knocked on the door to Aileen's flat. In one hand he held a bunch of roses, in the other an Indian takeaway, under his arm was a chilled bottle of champagne and in his trouser pocket, his mother's engagement ring.

The door opened and Aileen stood looking at him for a moment. 'Telford, where the bloody hell have you been?' she asked, before she threw her arms around him, pulled him inside and closed the door.

The Characters

Harry Lampeter - Anarchic urban adventurer and agent of the London Government.

Telford Stephenson - Agent of the Northern Alliance.

Martin Riley - Despised inventor of the bacterium that destroyed western civilisation.

Aileen Anderson - Chief mechanical engineer, Govan Shipbuilders, Glasgow.

Ms Rigby - Deputy Head of the Secret Intelligence Service.

'Shaky' Tom Fletcher - Drug dealer and companion to Harry Lampeter.

Brigadier Crisp - Discredited ex-chief of MI6, now working freelance.

Emma Crosby - Harry's childhood sweetheart.

Rosie - Landlady of the 'Bear and Penguin'

Elsa Nielson - Emma's lover.

Owen Turrell - Scottish Secret Intelligence Service agent.

PART FIVE

Two Autobiographical stories

BLIND FAITH

Published by Best of British Magazine 1st August 2016

In 1974, I was involved in a tour of rock concerts with a Dutch group called 'Focus.' At the time they were popular for their track, 'Hocus Pocus,' which involved falsetto singing and yodelling by the keyboard player, Thijs van Leer.

A few hours before the show, at Sheffield City Hall, Thijs decided that the grand piano was out of tune, so we sent for the City Hall piano tuner. George - not his real name - arrived by taxi soon after and quickly sorted the piano out to Thijs's satisfaction.

George, like most of the crew and performers, was in his mid-twenties. He used our 'hip' vernacular, but his short haircut and old-fashioned style of dress seemed rather out of place alongside our long hair and loon pants. I discovered that he was completely blind, lived with his mother, and it was she who chose his clothes and hairdresser.

The promoter asked me to drive George home, but I was dubious as I wasn't familiar with Sheffield. George announced that he would direct me, which did nothing to bolster my confidence, after all, how could a blind man take me through the centre of Sheffield? Having no choice, I escorted George out to the car park, helped him into my car, and we set off. The journey was to be one of the most surreal experiences of my life. George knew every turning, road sign, telephone pole and street light all the way from the city centre to his home on a small street in the suburbs. Wearing dark glasses and clutching his white stick with both hands, he faced me as he was giving directions. 'Do you see the street sign on the left with "A61 Barnsley" on it? Well, there's a turning to the right straight after the next lamp post. Quick, quick, you'll miss it, that's right,' was typical. He took charge during the trip and never hesitated. I have no idea how he could have done it, but we arrived at his house without a hitch.

When I got back, I told a couple of the roadies about my strange experience. One of the City Hall staffers had been listening, and she recounted another story about George.

He'd been called out a few months ago, just before one of Elton John's concerts; a fluctuation in temperature had put the piano out of tune. By the time George had finished tuning it, the audience were in their seats, waiting for the concert to start. Oblivious to them, because he was sitting behind the thick stage curtains, and concentrating on his work, George made a last check of the instrument by playing one of his favourite pieces, a Chopin nocturne called "Synthesia."

As he continued playing, one of the back-stage crew took it upon himself to open the curtains and, as they silently drew back, the blind piano tuner, dressed for the 1950s, white stick leaning against the piano, was revealed to the audience. He finished the nocturne, stood up, leaned over to wipe the keyboard with a duster, and heard the enthusiastic applause from an audience he had not realised could see him. Apparently, he took a nice bow, picked up his stick and tapped his way into the wings.

I envision Elton, splendidly spangled, standing smiling to one side of the stage, clapping him off. But I'm being fanciful: Elton was almost certainly in his dressing room, completely unaware of his warm-up act.

HEARTS OF OAK

Published by Best of British Magazine 1st Dec 2016

During the early 1980s, I was a technology teacher at Framingham Earl High School just outside Norwich. One of my classes was a group of disaffected teenage boys, who didn't much enjoy sitting still in the classroom, so, as often as I could, I took them out on trips in the school minibus. On one occasion, we went to a nearby timber yard, and the manager, a quiet man in his fifties, showed us around the site. The students were impressed by the big machines as they cut whole tree trunks into planks, before they were stacked for drying. It was very noisy but interesting. During a lull in the activity, the manager told us about an incident that had happened twenty years before.

'You never know what you'll find when you slice up a tree. We check all over with a metal detector for bolts, metal posts, wire, anything that the tree might have grown over. On the continent, they have all sorts of problems left over from the First World War, shells, shrapnel, bullets and the like. It depends on the age of the tree of course.'

The boys stood around paying vague attention.

'This one time our metal detector didn't find anything, but as we fed the tree into the big bandsaw to take a slice down its length, we discovered it was hollow. As the first rough plank fell away, bones spilled out: long bones, leg bones.'

Suddenly the boys were 'all ears.'

'We stopped the machine, I shone a torch into the cavity and there among the soft mulchy debris lay the rest of the skeleton, a human skeleton. We had no clue that the tree was hollow when we first craned it onto the saw bed, the opening at the top of the trunk had healed over years ago.

I called the police to report finding a body, but I knew they wouldn't be able to identify it. There were only a few scraps of cloth with it: everything else had rotted in the damp interior. A local PC came to take a look, and then a Scenes of Crime team came and removed the rest of the skeleton. They bagged it and took it away in a van.

Later we read in the paper that the medical examiner had found no obvious signs of trauma. No fractures of the skull for instance. They said the skeleton belonged to a male in his middle years at the time of his death, about a hundred years ago. But how the body got in there we never discovered.'

We left soon after and as I drove us back to school, I listened to the conversations behind me. There was no shortage of ideas, but what did 'sir' think?

'It was a cold winter's night,' I said. 'The man hadn't eaten for days, not since his last day of farm work up in North Norfolk. For the last few nights, he had been sleeping under hedges, damp and freezing. He'd been walking with rags binding his feet to tryt and keep out the cold. The dark came early but there was no shelter, no cow byre or shed, just the empty Norfolk landscape, flat and bleak and sere. The oak tree stood at the side of the road, and he saw the opening, up where the main branches divided. He climbed the ten feet up to it and lowered himself into the hollow trunk, among the dry leaves of the years. Finally, out of the cutting wind, he gradually warmed a little, then fell into a slumber from which he never woke.'

The boys pondered this briefly, but then the debate continued. Perhaps he was hiding in the tree? Was he a local who knew of the hollow trunk from boyhood expeditions? Was he hiding as part of a game? Did he find he couldn't climb out, got wedged in and nobody heard his shouts? Was he overcome once he climbed in? He might have suffocated or had a heart attack. The conversation batted back and forth.

Henry, the class dreamer, suddenly piped up. 'Perhaps somebody hid the body there. Perhaps a farmer came back from town unexpectedly and found the hired hand in bed with his wife. He could have dragged the man out into the yard by his hair and slit his throat with a trimming knife. Farmers always carry a knife stuck in their belt. He would have hidden the body, may be in an outhouse, and threatened his wife to make her keep quiet. Later, at dusk, maybe he carried it to the hollow tree on the edge of one of his fields and used a ladder or a rope to hoist it up to the opening and drop it inside. No one would be any the wiser and nobody would miss the man if he wasn't a local. If anybody asked, the farmer would just say he had run out of work, and the man had moved on.'

The group had listened in fascinated silence, but now the noisy debate began again. As we arrived back at the school, they agreed that Henry's was the likeliest explanation. Later, the art teacher told me that the story stimulated a whole series of gory masterpieces from the group.

How did the skeleton get into the tree? The truth is lost to history. But the boys of 4C always spoke of this as one of our better outings, and they bought me a box of chocolates at the end of the year, when I left to take up another post.

The End

If you have enjoyed the stories in this book, please consider leaving a short review on Amazon.

ACKNOWLEDGEMENTS

I would like to thank the following editors: Ion Newcombe at AntipodeanSF ezine, Iain Muir at Aphelion ezine, Crystalwizard at Altered Reality magazine, Simon Stabler at Best of British magazine, Dan Julian at Bull and Cross ezine, Nancy Kay Clark at CommuterLit ezine, Jamie Evans at Dark Dossier Magazine, Kenny B at Decasp ezine, Charley Fish at Fiction on the Web ezine, Hugh Cron, Diane Dickson and Nik Eveleigh at Literally Stories ezine, Lee Forman and Nina D'Arcangela at Pen of the Damned ezine, The Editors at Short-Story.Me ezine, Gloria Bobrowicz and Lee Forman at Sirens Call ezine, David Chang at Space Squid ezine, Alex Colvin at The Dirty Pool ezine, Brian Huggett at The Short Humour Site, and Stephen Smith at 365tomorrows ezine.

For the radio broadcasts, thanks to: Ion Newcombe on the Antipodean Radio Show and the staff at radio station 2NVR.

For the podcasts, thanks to: Mariah Avix at 600 Second Saga website.

For their encouragement and friendship thanks to: Sheila Ash, Sally East and Wally Smith, Tom Corbett and the Halesworth Library writers, and the Halesworth Cutting Edge writers.

Special thanks to my wife, Ann Walton, for her fine copy editing and constant support.

AUTHOR PAGE

Roger Ley was born and educated in London, and spent some of his formative years in Saudi Arabia. He worked as an engineer in the oilfields of North Africa and the North Sea, and later pursued a career in higher education.

Follow him on:

Facebook	https://www.facebook.com/rogerley2/
Twitter	https://twitter.com/RogerLey1
Website	http://rogerley.co.uk
Goodreads	Roger Ley

ALSO BY ROGER LEY

CHRONOSCAPE

A story of time travel and alternative history

Physicist, Martin Riley, has discovered a way to receive news stories from two weeks in the future but the Government steps in and cloaks the technology in secrecy. Despite Riley's warnings, politicians on both sides of the Atlantic make radical alterations to events. The first temporal alteration saves Princess Diana, the next saves the Twin Towers, but ripples travel far ahead and disturb Earth's future civilisation. The Timestream must be realigned, but at what cost?

A HORSE IN THE MORNING

Stories from a sometimes unusual life

Norwegian call girls, desert djinns and Berlin roof jumpers are just a sample of the characters that inhabit the pages of this collection of stories, some of which have been published in periodicals including: Reader's Digest, The Guardian and The Oldie, while others appear for the first time. It is the dramatic and amusing memoir of an engineer, teacher, and failed astronaut recounted with quirky British humour.

15079756R00125

Printed in Great Britain
by Amazon